T

2

DEAD WHERE YOU STAND!

Russ Conrad was a good man, tired of riding the rough edges of life, and Longbow Basin seemed a good place to settle. However, Fergus Keefer with his giant Slash K ranch was greedy for land, and wouldn't give a small rancher a chance — his hardcases saw to that. Guns and fists escalated to brushfires and murder. Now Conrad would have to fight for the peace and quiet he sought — but fighting was something he knew plenty about . . .

TYLER HATCH

---◆---

DEAD WHERE YOU STAND!

Complete and Unabridged

LINFORD
Leicester

First published in Great Britain in 2006 by
Robert Hale Limited
London

First Linford Edition
published 2007
by arrangement with
Robert Hale Limited
London

British Library CIP Data

Hatch, Tyler
  Dead where you stand!.—Large print ed.—
  Linford western library
  1. Ranching—Fiction 2. Western stories
  3. Large type books
  I. Title
  823.9'14 [F]

ISBN 978–1–84617–813–9

Published by
F. A. Thorpe (Publishing)
Anstey, Leicestershire

Set by Words & Graphics Ltd.
Anstey, Leicestershire
Printed and bound in Great Britain by
T. J. International Ltd., Padstow, Cornwall

This book is printed on acid-free paper

1

THIS LAND IS MINE

This land would do him fine, Russ Conrad decided, leaning on to the saddlehorn and lifting slightly in the stirrups to better see below the rocky ledge where he sat his roan.

Yes, pretty rugged, with a couple of draws visible and the rise of timber-clad hills in a small range. There was water, a long, bendy creek or two short ones, continuity or separation being blocked from his view by a boulderfield. Sweeping right he saw the rise where he would build his cabin, with a convenient flat grassy section that would suit corrals. He could build a root cellar into the slope behind the cabin site and, later, when it became necessary, a barn across from the corral. This would necessitate some digging and levelling but that was what he was prepared for.

He was about to become a small-time rancher in Longbow Basin, and it was a good feeling. A *fine* feeling.

'Like the view?'

The voice was deep, not unfriendly, but not friendly, either. Conrad, tall in the saddle and loose-limbed, turned towards the speaker. Two men sat horses above his ledge, cowmen by the looks of their clothes. They had saddleguns and cartridge belt rigs about their waists but their hands were holding reins. The biggest one, the speaker, had tufts of unruly fair hair showing beneath his sweat-stained hat, a face that had been close to a few too many fists, and very blue eyes with a steely glint. The second man was average in every way that Conrad could judge, darker, narrow-faced, with restless eyes and a mean mouth.

'Yeah,' Conrad said, in answer to the question. 'Right fine quarter-section.'

'Who said there's a quarter-section down there?' the big one asked crisply.

Conrad tapped his saddle-bag. 'Survey map. Picked one up in town. Clerk shaded in this quarter-section as being still available.'

'Well, it ain't.' Very definite. 'You see the cattle down at the creek? Small lean-to and campfire set-up — through the brush there?'

Conrad frowned slightly. He was deep-tanned from long drifting trails, body lean and hard-muscled. Unshaven right now, but normally with clean jowls. His nose was slightly flattened above the wide mouth, and the eyes were hazel, seeking the big man's now. Without speaking, he started to undo the flap of the saddle-bag. The riders tensed, the smaller one dropping a hand to his Colt's butt. The big one just tightened his grip on the reins.

'Noticed the cows,' he admitted. 'Quite a few, but took 'em for strays.'

He brought out the folded survey map, checked the oblong fold facing him and looked up, shaking his head slowly. 'Map shows it as being available all right.'

'Hell with the map, feller, I told you it's not available.' The big rider was leaning forward now, piercing blue eyes holding steady on Conrad. 'You're on Slash K here.'

'A name I've heard. Someone named Keefer runs it?'

'Fergus Keefer,' the big rider confirmed. 'Biggest spread in the basin and ready to get bigger. A lot bigger. Which is why this land ain't for prove-up, or sale, or anythin' else. You might's well ride on.' He pointed to the distant hills. 'Open range yonder.'

Conrad half hipped in the saddle, pursed his lips. 'Be a long way from town — I like it here better.'

The dark man swore softly, but looked to his companion for a lead. The blue eyes were ice-cold now, studying. 'On the prod, huh?'

'Not by a damn sight. I'm looking for peace and quiet, a place to build up, rear a family eventually, I guess

— friend of mine proved-up here in the basin a spell back — Reece? Charley Reece?'

The dark man hawked and spat, snorting. The big one narrowed his eyes and nodded slowly. 'He mentioned he'd written someone about how good it was in the basin and hoped his friend would turn up — that's you, huh?'

'Yeah — Russ Conrad.'

The big one nodded. 'I'm Chick Brodie.' He jerked his head. 'Sidekick is Dog Beale. We work for Mr Keefer. He bought out your friend Reece some time back.'

Conrad tensed. 'Charley's gone from the basin?'

'No — he's still here.'

Dog Beale laughed shortly. 'Find him in town. On the rise at the north end.'

Conrad tensed. The only thing he had seen at the north end of town on the rise there was — 'Boot Hill?' They stared back, keeping their faces expressionless. 'The hell happened?'

'Got drunk on what Keefer paid him

for his dirt, picked a fight and it ended in guns.'

'Not Charley Reece! He was no trouble-making drunk! He'd cross the street rather than pick a fight.'

Brodie shrugged, his look challenging. 'Well, I guess that's what he shoulda done.'

'Who killed him?'

'Feller he picked a fight with.' Brodie smiled crookedly and Dog laughed again.

Conrad felt his face tighten, boring his gaze into Brodie. 'You?'

'Aw, shucks — ' He lifted a hand quickly. 'Now, don't go gettin' riled, Conrad! It were all fair-an'-square. Most of the town seen it. I din' want to draw on him, but he wouldn't back off.'

'Or you wouldn't let him.' Conrad held the man's gaze a few moments longer, then lifted his reins and turned the roan down-slope towards the trail to town.

'Hey, Conrad! You're goin' the wrong way.' Brodie flapped a hand at the hills.

'That way yonder takes you outa the basin.'

Conrad didn't answer or turn, just kept riding. Dog Beale drew his rifle from the scabbard but Brodie said, without turning, 'Put it away — there's been enough shootin'.'

★   ★   ★

The same woman clerk was behind the counter in the Land Agency when Conrad walked through the door, dusty from the fast ride in from the basin. She was fair-haired, with a blue ribbon drawing her hair back from her oval face. She wore a blue-and-white gingham dress and he guessed she was in her twenties, maybe at the high end. There was a name on a small board across the section of counter where she worked over a leather-bound ledger. *Miss Ali Tyrell*. She looked up, waited until he came right in and wasn't just silhouetted against the glare of the street. She smiled as she recognized him from his previous visit.

'Oh, Mr Conrad, I didn't expect you back so soon. You did say you would stay out overnight and inspect the quarter-section thoroughly. Not to your satisfaction?'

He doffed his hat, ran a hand through thick sweaty dark curls and smiled briefly. 'Land's fine — welcome committee was a little unexpected, though.'

Her face straightened and he saw genuine concern in her grey eyes. 'Keefer's men?'

'Someone named Brodie and Beale . . . you forgot to mention Keefer is interested in that land.'

She flushed. 'I'm sorry. Chick Brodie is a watchdog for Fergus Keefer. Dog Beale hangs around with him most of the time. There wasn't any . . . trouble?'

Conrad shook his head. 'Just a little talk of it. There're cows grazing and a temporary building and camp. That's why Brodie said the section isn't available.'

'Well, he's wrong! Keefer's not supposed to be using that land! He's like most of the big ranchers who started on open range. They think wherever there's land they can move in and that's an end to it. They've ignored the government survey and still consider they rule the roost. Keefer hasn't filed any claim, so that quarter-section's still open for six-month prove-up. From the details you gave me earlier, all you need to do is fill in the file form and it's yours.'

He hesitated, set his hat on the counter. 'Could you fill it in for me?' She frowned but nodded, and he added, embarrassed, 'I . . . don't write so good. Can sort of scratch my name, but you'd have to be pretty good to make it out.'

'Of course, it won't be any trouble,' she said pleasantly, reaching for a box under the counter and taking out a printed form. 'Do you want to do it now?'

'If you're sure the land's still up, yeah.'

'I'm sure.' She began to ask him a few questions about places he had worked, trail bosses who could give him a reference, any army service — 'Sure. *Didn't everyone fight in the War?*' She smiled without showing it, keeping her head down as she wrote. She felt a little sorry for this ranny. Not that he looked the type to want any sympathy, too independent for that, but there were so many men who were almost completely illiterate. Sent out to work before their age reached double figures, no time for schooling or very little, and then the War and they came back, hardened, faced a life where reading and writing skills were of growing importance. And they were skills they didn't have . . .

At least he had the courage to admit it, though she bet silently that he had hidden his handicap well enough for a long time. It would only be in unavoidable situations like this where he would have to admit it.

She turned the form around towards him and handed him a pen, pointing to

10

a line near the bottom. 'Sign there, Mr Conrad, please.'

He held the pen awkwardly and scratched something that might have deciphered to *Russell Conrad* with a little effort and a lot of imagination. She saw he was flushed slightly and smiled to put him at his ease.

'There, you are now officially tenant on a quarter-section of Conifer County land in Longbow Basin. If you prove-up on it by the deadline, in six months' time, the title will fully revert to you, courtesy of the government.'

He smiled and couldn't hide the pride and excitement in his face. 'Waited a long time for this. Kept putting it off. Going from job to job, spending all my money like a fool, not giving the future a thought.'

'Well, your future awaits you now — it's whatever you want to make of it, Mr Conrad.' His smile widened and he nodded, folded the claim and put it in his shirt pocket. But she saw he had sobered now. 'Look, don't worry about

Fergus Keefer. He's a big-wig around here and likes to think he can do what he likes but the laws are stronger now and being enforced. He has to realize that he can't ride roughshod over everyone, just as he pleases, like he has been doing.'

'Yeah. Seems he did it to an army buddy of mine — Charley Reece.'

She frowned. 'He was your friend . . . ? I'm sorry. But Charley got drunk and — '

'I don't believe that,' he cut in sharply. 'Charley liked a drink and a wingding at trail's end but he wasn't quarrelsome. He'd have to be prodded into a gunfight.'

Hesitant, she said, 'Well, if Chick Brodie wants to argue, there's no backing-out, I'm afraid.'

'Was it a fair square-off?' he asked grimly.

'Ye-es — I have to say that. It happened right outside here in the street. Charley went for his gun first, but I also have to say that Chick Brodie goaded him into it, wouldn't let up so

12

that there was no other way for it to end but in a gunfight.'

'Why? He told me Keefer had bought Charley out. What was the beef with Brodie?'

Ali Tyrell sighed. 'Chick is a roughneck. He can hold his liquor when he wants. But he's a man of moods. When he's quarrelsome, he'll have his fight and someone will be sorry. It's never been Chick Brodie so far.' She paused and added quietly, 'Then again, he does whatever Keefer tells him.'

Conrad frowned. 'Keefer wanted Charley dead?'

'I don't know, only that Brodie is Keefer's trouble-shooter.'

'Did he pay Charley a fair price?'

'Fair as far as Keefer is concerned.'

'Then Charley was crowded into selling.'

She straightened. 'I . . . can't comment on that, Mr Conrad. If you'll take my advice you'll lodge that land claim with the bank for safe keeping.'

'Thanks, I'll do that. Keefer can't

make any claim on my land now?'

'None whatsoever — unless, of course, you don't prove-up by the deadline. But he doesn't need that land — he was just looking to the future expansion of Slash K, kept an eye on it. But he didn't file on it and you did, so good luck.'

Conrad nodded his thanks and stepped outside into the heat and glare of the street. He set his hat on his head and then paused. Chick Brodie and Dog Beale were leaning on the hitch rail, smoking. Brodie gave him a crooked smile.

'So you had to go and do it, huh? Just had to file on that land I told you Mr Keefer wanted.'

'That land is mine, Brodie.' Conrad tapped his shirt pocket and Brodie flicked his still burning cigarette against his shirt front. 'Signed and sealed — all I have to do is deliver in six months' time.'

'A lot can happen in six months.'

'I won't argue with you there.'

'Lemme show you what *could* happen — '

And Brodie launched himself off the hitch rail straight at Conrad, big fists balled-up and swinging.

Russ Conrad had been keyed-up since stepping out of the Land Agency and was ready. His hands flashed up in front of his face as Brodie swung. The big man's fist was caught in a work-hardened palm, twisted, and Conrad's other arm rose and parried the second blow.

He wrenched harder and Brodie grunted in pain and staggered to one side. He came surging back but Dog Beale yelled something, momentarily distracting Brodie, and then Conrad's six-gun crashed across the side of the man's head. Brodie stopped in his tracks, arms dropping to his sides, his jaw hanging slackly as his eyes stared, then rolled up into their sockets as his legs gave way.

He was still settling in the dust when Beale jumped over the hitch rail, dragging at his pistol as he ran at Conrad. The drifter dropped in a slide, crashing his boots against Dog's knee-caps. The man howled and fell to his throbbing knees. Conrad was up in a flash and gun-whipped him to the dust alongside the unconscious Brodie.

Men were running down the street but a small crowd had already gathered and stood looking from the gun-whipped men to Russ Conrad. Ali Tyrell was standing in the doorway of the agency, one hand to her mouth, a frown puckering her smooth face.

Then the crowd opened out and a young man wearing a star pushed his way through. He was almost as tall as Conrad, but younger and not as broad. He had a boyish face but there was a hardness in his eyes and jaw that gave Conrad pause as he holstered his Colt.

'Sheriff Brad Tyrell,' the man said curtly. 'Who the hell're you and what do you think you're doing?'

'Defending myself, Sheriff.'

Tyrell's jaw jutted and then Ali spoke

from the doorway. 'He's right, Brad. He'd just left the office and was walking to his mount when Chick Brodie went for him.'

Tyrell looked at Ali, nodded gently, and looked around at the crowd. 'Anyone else see it?' Several men said they did and Tyrell again looked at the woman. 'OK, Sis — thanks for your help . . . and you'd be who, mister?'

Conrad told him. 'Just signed on to prove-up on a quarter-section but Brodie said Keefer had his eye on it.'

Tyrell frowned. 'Means he hadn't filed on it?' He lifted his gaze once more to his sister. Ali shook her head. 'All right, Conrad. But you keep your gun leathered when you're in my town. That's the rule.'

'Sounds like a good idea, Sheriff. Pity you didn't make Brodie do it the day he killed Charley Reece.'

The lawman bristled. 'You worry about stickin' to the law yourself! Never mind about what's happened in the past. Dunno as I like a man who has to defend himself with his gun against someone comin' at him with just his fists.'

'I've got work to do, proving-up. I didn't aim to bust my hands on a knothead like Brodie — nor Dog Beale.'

Tyrell poked a stiffened finger in Conrad's face. 'You just watch it! If either of these two has a cracked skull, you'll see the inside of my jailhouse!'

'Wouldn't be the first,' Conrad told him easily. 'Now, if you're finished, *Sheriff*, I've got business at the bank and some stores to buy.'

Tyrell didn't like it but jerked his head and Conrad stepped around him, untied the roan's reins and led it through the crowd down the street.

The small crowd dispersed and the sheriff stepped up on to the walk beside his sister. 'That feller's trouble, Sis.'

'I don't know, Brad. I think mostly he's a man who's prepared to stand up for what he believes is right.'

Tyrell smiled ruefully. 'They can be the very worst kind!'

2

MAVERICKS

He knew they were watching him.

Day after day when he went into the Catamount Hills and felled trees for his cabin, dragging the stripped trunks back to his worksite on a sled he had made. There they were: up on the slopes, sitting out in the open, studying him through field-glasses, making no attempt to hide.

That was OK with Conrad: he had nothing to hide. All he wanted to do was build his cabin and get that part of the prove-up out of the way. Not only that, but it would give him shelter and he knew he would need it before the six months were up. It was already near the end of July, and the heat would soon fade night and early morning in this basin, colder air sweeping in.

It wasn't the first cabin he had built: he had put in almost a year once working with a man who hired out his carpentering talents, building cabins and root cellars and barns. Making a few dollars, too, but mighty hard work.

But Conrad wasn't afraid of using his muscles, kind of enjoyed it. He lost a lot of sweat and some poundage, honed right down to muscle and tendon, slept well, ate meagrely. But he knew he would have to have more meat in his diet if he was to keep up this pace and get the place the way he wanted by deadline.

He shot a couple of deer, the carcass of one raided by a big cat in the Catamount Hills one night after he had dressed it out and hung it in a tree to bleed out properly. He saw the cat moving at speed through the trees, noticing the swollen dugs of a female — which might mean there were kittens someplace close by — admired the rippling coat as the muscles and steel-spring tendons stretched and compressed. Slowly, he lowered his rifle. It had to eat, too. But he was more careful with his own bounty after that. He had neither time nor energy to waste shooting something for grub only to lose it to some prowling mountain lion, mother or not.

There were cattle roaming his section, too. Unbranded mostly, yearlings. Mavericks, likely Keefer's, but with the unwritten law of an unbranded animal being fair game for whoever came across it, he knew he didn't have to use good working time hunting in the Catamounts. He could shoot one of the mavericks and dress it out for the meat his hardworking body craved.

He was frying some steak for breakfast one morning, the savoury odour and hissing of the meat in the skillet filling the fireplace he had made in front of his growing cabin with a fine mouth-watering smoke. Because of the crackling of the steak in the grease and the few wild onions and a couple of potatoes he had been saving also cooking, he didn't hear the horsemen.

When someone said, 'That smells mighty good,' he jumped straight for the rifle leaning against a log. But his hand froze on the breech as a gun fired and dust spurted close by.

Four horsemen sat their mounts on the area he was levelling for the barn-to-be. He recognized Brodie and Dog Beale, didn't know the other two but bet himself the slab-bodied man in the good quality range clothes and with silver grey hair showing under his cream Stetson was Fergus Keefer himself.

The other three still holding their rifles on him, Conrad stood slowly. 'S'pose I should be neighbourly and ask you to join me for breakfast.'

Keefer, his triangular face relaxed and with a smile just touching his thin lips, lifted a hand from his lap and waved it side to side. 'Already eaten — likely some of the same steak you're cooking. Or a relative to it.'

Conrad knew what the man was

saying. 'No brand on this beef, Mr Keefer. There's the hide hanging from that low limb. Kept it in case.'

'In case of what?'

Conrad waved a hand around at the armed trio. 'Something like this.'

'You know damn well that's Slash K beef!' growled Brodie. The swelling on his face hadn't yet gone down properly since the gun-whipping and it gave him a lopsided brutish look. 'We got mavericks all over these slopes!'

'Mavericks, sure — means they ain't branded and fair game for anyone who can take 'em.'

'You believe that?' Keefer asked quietly.

Conrad smiled crookedly. 'I'd like to. Specially right now.'

Keefer shook his head slowly. 'Not a chance. You took this land from under my nose, mister, and that's all I'll allow — and only that because it's on legal papers. You leave my beef be. I'll give you this one warning.'

The rancher started to swing his

horse around and Conrad bent to the skillet and turned the steak. Then Brodie's rifle crashed and the skillet rang dully as it flew from Conrad's grasp and he jumped back to avoid the hot grease. Some burnt his wrist and forearm, splashed his clothes. The steak was lying in the fire, charring. Some of the grease sputtered and flared. Beale and the other cowboy, named Todd, laughed. Keefer looked faintly amused. Brodie's look was hopefully challenging.

'Put that on my slate, Chick,' Conrad said, and Brodie's smirk slowly disappeared. He flicked his blue eyes to Keefer who shook his head just once.

It was enough and Brodie's lips tightened. 'There'll come a time, drifter.'

'Say when,' Conrad replied but Keefer cut in.

'You want to eat my beef, Conrad, you pay for it. My men're watching you, keeping tally. This one I give you for free. From now on every maverick you kill will cost you ten dollars.' Keefer meant it.

'Might have trouble collecting.'

Keefer shook his head, smiling, turned his horse and rode back down the slope. Brodie and the others followed.

Conrad recovered the skillet, ruined by the bullet. He tossed it aside, went to the shade where he had a haunch of beef under a damp gunnysack and cut off two slabs. He threaded them on a sharpened stick and squatted in front of the fire, holding them in the flames. Might as well eat well while he could.

He knew there would be some sort of a penalty to pay for the next side of beef he claimed.

★   ★   ★

They left him alone for several weeks although he knew they were watching. He also noticed that the number of mavericks usually wandering the brush and timber on Catamount Hill had dwindled, which likely meant that Keefer's men were driving them back on to Slash K land. He had seen riders several times.

But he couldn't argue with Keefer, maybe might make something of his men trespassing, but that was kid-stuff and could get him tied-up in the courts which meant work would fall behind. It could be that was Keefer's plan, testing him, seeing if he would work to the letter of the law or try to do something about any hassles himself.

Conrad wanted those mavericks. Not all. He wasn't going to be greedy, but a small herd of about a hundred would clinch things when it came to prove-up assessment. Keefer wouldn't miss them: he had thousands roaming his vast ranges. But Keefer was here first and he had that stubbornness and wasn't about to give one Southern inch, even though he must know by Conrad's accent that his neighbour was from Texas.

No. Keefer was the big frog in this pool and although he had been pleasant enough that time he had caught Conrad cooking Slash K beef, there was an arrogance about him. And a cold ruthlessness that showed through the veneer.

Conrad also sensed an indifference to anything and anyone Keefer had no direct use for.

Come the pinch, and Keefer would cut loose Brodie and Dog Beale and to hell with the consequences.

He saw all this coming and was ready for it in one way — keeping his guns handy while he worked, getting up at night for a ride around the boundaries. But it was all a damn nuisance. There was no open threat, but a threat was there, unspoken, just the same.

His work was not only falling behind, but he needed help with the heavy logs as the walls of the cabin began to grow. So he took time off and rode into town, found himself hitching his horse to the rail outside the Land Agency. He went in, aware of his grubby clothes and his smell: stale sweat and smoke. He hadn't taken time off for a decent wash in the creek yet. There were dead leaves and bits of bark in his beard and Ali Tyrell studied him warily as he approached. Then her face brightened.

'Oh, it's you, Mr Conrad! I hardly recognized you.'

He doffed his hat and turned it between his calloused fingers. 'Sorry for the way I look, ma'am. Kinda busy and only myself to worry about. Guess by the looks of folk I passed on the street, I don't smell like roses, either.'

She smiled. 'We-ell, I daresay I've smelled worse.' Then there was a mischievous look in her grey eyes as she added, 'Can't quite remember when, or where, though . . . '

He laughed briefly. 'No — well, I ain't staying long. But what I wanted to ask, do you know of someone I could hire for a few days to help me with the walls of my cabin? I've got 'em as high as I can manage alone, using ropes and sapling slides, but now I need that extra boost, and there's the roof-frame, too.

Can't pay much, but there'll be beefsteak for breakfast and supper.'

She looked at him sharply then. 'Slash K beef?'

'Maverick beef,' he corrected her.

'Well, just . . . go easy, if you don't mind a warning. Keefer has been talking with Brad, not laying any official complaint, but making it plain he figures those mavericks belong to him and if you take the occasional one for food — well, he's a powerful and dangerous man.'

'Yeah, so he tells me. But it's still the law of the range, an unbranded calf or steer is for the taking.'

'Not from Keefer's range. Your friend Reece found that out.' She shut off abruptly, realizing she had said too much. Conrad's eyes narrowed and before he could speak, she said, 'There's no way it can be proved, but — well, Keefer's price for Charley Reece's land wasn't all that fair.'

'Recollect you said it was 'fair for Keefer'. Should've listened closer. You were trying to tell me, huh?'

She nodded, sighed. 'The word was that Charley, with some whiskey under his belt, decided to even things up a little.'

'And throw a wide loop over Keefer's steers?'

'So Keefer claimed. Brad looked into it but it was never proved. Never disproved, either.'

'And Keefer couldn't let anyone think Charley had gotten away with it so turned Brodie loose on him . . . ?'

She looked uncomfortable. 'It seems a possibility.'

Conrad nodded gently. 'I'll remember that, but right now I need a hand with raising my cabin.'

'Of course. I do know of someone who might help you out. He's a young drifter hanging around town waiting for his friend who's on some sort of trail drive down in Mexico. He's been asking about land; maybe he and his friend are thinking of settling here. But Randy McLaren was swamping out the saloon earlier, so I know he's short of money.'

'Sounds OK — thanks.'

'Glad to help.' She smiled but let it fade slowly. 'Please don't underestimate Fergus Keefer, Mr Conrad.'

At the door he said, 'Don't aim to — and the name's Russ.' He nodded, as he set his hat on his head and went out.

He found McLaren stacking crates behind the saloon, a rangy young *hombre* who yet had the look of a man who had been around and seen plenty. He was a veteran trail driver.

'I don't like towns much, except on a Sat'd'y night or end of a drive,' McLaren said. He had sandy hair and light fuzz that passed for stubble, almost lost amongst the freckles on his face. 'Rather work out in the open. Seventy cents a day's OK by me. We goin' now?'

'If you're ready. Get your outfit while I pick up a coupla things at the general store.'

They agreed to meet at the bridge over the creek and Conrad purchased a new chisel and an oilstone, a file for sharpening his axe, two spare hickory handles, a small keg of nails, some flour and a small bag of coffee beans.

Randy was a good worker and also knew what he was about. He didn't go by any clock, either. He started a job and if it was possible he wanted to get it done, even if it meant working after dark. He was good with a hammer and chisel, cut better, tighter-fitting notches in the log ends than Conrad could manage.

'Feel like I'm short-changing you,' Conrad allowed one evening, as they worked by firelight, notching roof frames.

Randy shrugged, grinning with his large teeth. A couple of the front ones were crossed over, his mouth too crowded, and he admitted they gave him problems at times.

'Coupla mouthfuls of red-eye helps, though,' he added. At Conrad's wary look he said, 'Hell, I don't get drunk when I'm working, Russ! Trail's end and Sat'd'y nights are different. But I'm sober on the job.'

'I've got no complaints, Randy. C'mon, let's knock off and I'll cook us up a steak and try not to burn a batch of biscuits.'

'O-K! Belly tells me I'm about ready for somethin'. You trust me to boil some of them coffee beans you brung?'

'Go ahead.'

It was a rough, outdoor meal, the steaks somewhat charred, greasy and even a little tough, although they came from a maverick calf. The biscuits had acquired a very dark brown crust that was bordering on black and Randy's coffee was typical trail java — strong enough to float a horseshoe.

But they had good appetites and laughed about it, smoked contentedly afterwards and turned in.

They had the roof frame up by noon next day and Conrad set about splitting shingles. Randy climbed up and stacked the finished ones in piles at the corners where they wouldn't slide off, ready for attaching later. From up there, he shaded his eyes and looked around, then said, when he saw Conrad straightening stiffly and massaging his back, 'Some nice-lookin' cows down there in that dry wash — bunch of six or seven. I could round 'em up and we could keep 'em in that small draw behind where you figure to build your barn. Be a shame to pass 'em up, Russ. A damn shame.'

Conrad rolled a cigarette and tossed up tobacco sack and papers to McClaren. 'Figured I might leave the gathering of a herd till I get the cabin finished and corrals set up. It's going to cause trouble with Keefer and I'd like to be well advanced towards prove-up before that happens.'

'You're the boss — pity though. I could make you a brandin' iron and once you've got your mark on 'em, ain't a lot Keefer can do.'

Conrad looked sharp, frowned as he smoked. 'We'll leave it for now.'

'You got a brand in mind?' Randy pushed.

Conrad nodded slowly. 'Just figured

to call the place Bar C. Nothin' fancy.'

'Hell, that's a breeze to make a brandin' iron for. Show you when I come down if we can find a length of rod.'

Of course, Randy did a fine, fast job and Conrad knew he was weakening. In the end he compromised. If the mavericks were still there when they finished wiring on the shingles that afternoon, they'd bring them in.

'And brand 'em,' Randy added and, hesitating briefly, Conrad nodded.

But he had a feeling that this was going to be the beginning of a heap of trouble.

3

NEIGHBOURS

It was dark before they had the seven mavericks rounded-up and driven into the small draw, not far from the cabin. This latter was looking well now, the shingles tied on, the walls erected. No door yet and shutters were needed on the windows but it was coming along fine.

Conrad was already thinking ahead to the corrals and barn, wondered if McLaren would be willing to stay on a little longer — probably not. He was worried about his pard, someone named Ringo Magraw, and was talking about going on down to Mexico to look for him.

It was hard, slogging, dirty work branding these wild cattle, used to free-roaming and now confined in the draw with a brush fence across the entrance. There was a lot of dust and bawling and the stink of singed hide. Both men had bruises from butts and flailing hoofs but they were happy with their work as Conrad kicked dirt over the branding fire.

'A little bit of history, Randy. You've taken part in the beginnings of a new cattle empire. The mighty Bar C!'

'I have?' Randy blinked.

Conrad shrugged as he smiled slowly. 'A man can dream, I guess. No, I don't have ambitions to try to outclass men like Keefer, but I aim to build up a decent-sized spread over the years.'

'Wish you luck. Look, Russ, I'm still worried about my pard, Ringo. He can be a mite wild and they were runnin' steers through *bandido* country he said . . . guess I'll have to be movin' along, see if I can find him. You can manage now.'

Conrad nodded, mopping sweat and smearing dirt on his face. 'Be sorry to see you leave, Randy. You and your pard want to look in on me when you get back, be glad to see you.'

They shook hands after breakfast and it was still grey, not yet quite light. 'Russ, been good knowin' you. Me an' Ringo'll look in and spend a few days helpin' out if we can.'

'Just come and say howdy is fine. Ride easy, Randy.'

'You, too.'

He mounted his shaggy dun and rode off down the slope and headed into the Catamount Hills. Conrad sat on a rock, smoking, watching him go. He would sure miss that ranny.

Later, he took the breakfast things down to the creek and washed them, scrubbing the platters with sand. Rinsing, he thought he heard horses above the splash of water over the rocks and clatter of utensils. Still squatting, he looked over his shoulder . . . and froze.

There were four riders in front of the cabin — his rifle was inside there — and he knew he was in trouble. They were armed and the six-gun he was wearing had been pushed carelessly around towards his back while he scrubbed dishes.

Chick Brodie grinned down at him from atop his big brown mount with one chewed ear. 'Mornin', Conrad. We lost track of some mavericks yest'y, last seen headin' for a dry wash yonder. Now we find their tracks up here. And a bunch of cows just like 'em in a draw behind us.'

'*Branded* cows,' Conrad corrected him, rising slowly. 'Wearing my Bar C on their hides now.'

'That right? Bar C . . . must be a new brand hereabouts. Never heard of it before and I guess it ain't gonna be one I'll hear much about again.'

'Wouldn't bet on it, Chick.'

'I would.' Brodie gestured to his riders and Dog Beale brought his rifle into view. 'Walk on up here, Conrad. We got a few things to discuss . . . '

There was a call from down-slope, at the foot of Catamount Hill, and Conrad saw a rider waving his hat.

Brodie grinned tightly.

'We're gonna have company.'

Two riders came out of the brush, leading a shaggy dun. Randy McLaren was slumped loosely in the saddle, hands tied to the horn.

Brodie laughed. 'You should see your face! — OK boys, time to get this party goin'.'

He dismounted and pulled on a pair of begrimed leather work gloves, never taking his eyes off Conrad who was slowly walking up the slope, hands balling into fists.

Rifle barrels followed his every move.

* * *

Brad Tyrell was just opening his office door, yawning, when a dusty rider on a piebald that had seen hard trails, hauled rein and lifted a hand.

'Hey, Sheriff! Just the man I want to see. Lookin' for a pard of mine, Randy McLaren. Lanky streak of misery, sandy hair — '

'Not here,' the sheriff cut in. 'He's been workin' out at Catamount Hill, helpin' a settler put up a cabin.'

The rider took off his hat and scratched at his sweaty scalp. He was weathered dark as a rifle stock, had squinty eyes like a man who spends a lot of time in deserts. His squarish face was beard-shaggy and dirty. 'Well, that's Randy for you, likes buildin' things. Put a hammer in his hand and he'll throw you up a barn or a cabin or a set of corrals before sundown — almost, anyways. How do I find this Catamount place?'

Brad Tyrell hesitated a little. 'You're who?'

'Ringo Magraw. Been ridin' drag on a bunch of longhorns down Durango way. Dry as a handful of autumn leaves most times, but damned if we din' get caught in a flash flood. Rain up in the sierras they say. Marooned for nigh on a week, then it was bogs, an' they dried an' — Randy musta been wonderin' what'd happened to me.'

41

'Yeah, he did mention his pard was overdue. Listen, I've got to go out there. A little . . . legal problem. You want to come in and grab a cup of java with me, we can ride out together.'

Ringo was already dismounting. 'Suits me. Say, you wouldn't have a slug of redeye to add to the coffee, would you? Mouth's all puckered from that blamed tequila . . . '

★   ★   ★

Conrad, a rifle muzzle poking hard into his midriff, looked past Dog Beale who was holding the gun to where a sweating Brodie was shaking one of his gloved hands, the leather now all stained with blood and bits of flesh. Conrad's face was bruised and cut, one eye swelling. Brodie had started in on him, swinging, driving brutal blows into Conrad's body, then changed his mind and turned to the helpless Randy McLaren being held by two hard-eyed cowpokes.

'Drifter, I guess I gotta teach you that you don't come into Slash K territory and help its enemies — OK? Sorry about this . . . '

Then he had administered one of the worst and bloodiest beatings Conrad had ever seen a man take. Arms working like pistons, Brodie had smashed blow after blow into Randy's lean body; then worked on his face, the leather making muffled, sliding sounds as it tore and bruised flesh, smashed lips against teeth that were loosened in their gums. A mix of blood and sweat fanned-out around Randy's head.

Conrad had bucked and fought to get free from the men holding him but in vain. His efforts had only earned him a couple of blows from Dog's rifle butt and finally his legs had buckled and he had fallen to his knees, glaring hatred at the grunting Brodie. Only when the battered and bloody Randy McLaren lay unconscious, did Brodie stop to draw breath and glare challengingly at Conrad. He smirked at the impotent settler and, holding the man's gaze, drove his boot heels down brutally on to Randy's limp hands. Bones crunched. Then he kicked the prone man hard in the head. Twice.

'You miserable bastard, Brodie! When they turn me loose, you're dead where you stand!'

'No one's gonna turn you loose, knothead.'

Conrad paused, the murderous fury plain on his face in the narrowed eyes, the flaring nostrils and bitten-down lip line now as thin as a razor slash. 'So you're not finished with me, yet.'

'Not by a damn sight!' Brodie grinned crookedly, a happy man now. 'Luck of the draw, I guess.' He adjusted his gloves and started forward. 'Bad luck — and all yours.'

Suddenly Dog Beale jumped as Conrad's arm swept up, knocking the rifle aside, and he leapt to his feet, stepped forward and drove a knee into Dog's crotch. The man went down fast, moaning sickly. All the men except the two who had held Randy while Brodie beat him, were mounted again now, slow to make a move. Brodie himself was taken by surprise.

Conrad scooped up the rifle and Brodie was already diving behind the line of mounted men, yelling, 'Stop that son of a bitch!'

The men were well trained and jumped their mounts forward. Conrad stumbled as he leapt back, triggered the rifle wildly. It scattered the men but they rode in again and Conrad had to plunge down the slope to keep from being ridden down. Brodie was yelling and swearing as he tore off his gloves and stuffed them inside his shirt, running for his own horse.

Conrad fell again, rolled into the creek, lunged up and waded out into midstream. Two horsemen plunged their mounts in after him and although he triggered another rifle shot, he was crushed between the two heaving mounts. He lost the gun, went under, ribs creaking from the impact of the horses. Needing air, he rolled and thrashed wildly in the muddy water in an effort to dodge the stomping hoofs that rattled like muffled drumbeats on the creekbed rocks.

He came up out of the creek, gasping, water's silver mixed with mud streaming from his face and body, right alongside one of the Slash K men. It was pure luck and he reacted instinctively, grabbing the man and yanking him violently out of the saddle. The man yelled and then he was sinking, muddy water gushing down his throat. The second rider came in shooting, but afraid of hitting his pard, threw the shot wild.

Conrad, fighting to hold the wet reins of the plunging horse, slammed it into the other and the horses tangled and shrilled as their legs thrashed the water to foam. The Slash K man swiped at Conrad with his six-gun. The sodbuster ducked under the arm, twisted the gun from the other's grip, then slammed it back-handed into the man's face.

He was still going down over his mount's rump when Conrad shouldered him off and leapt into the saddle. Keeping the horse between him and the bank where Brodie was screaming in frustration, he fired the Colt once. They shot back, leery of hitting their own man for a few moments. Then Conrad's mount heaved up on the far bank and, lying low over the animal's arched neck, he crashed into the brush and raced for the shelter of the timber on Catamount Hill.

Bullets zipped and buzzed all round him, tearing at leaves and twigs. He zigzagged the frightened horse under him and at last was lost amongst the trees. He kept going, six-gun rammed into his belt now, weaving the mount up the slope.

Brodie was beside himself, spittle flying, mixing curses and wild orders, the cowboys trying to figure out just what the hell he wanted them to do. They all figured he would want Conrad run down so they plunged across the creek, one man falling into the path of other mounts behind, causing a melee. By the time it was sorted out, Brodie was on the far bank, standing in stirrups, cursing them all.

'Goddamnit! We had him — had him cold! And now he's gone! Todd, get back to the ranch and tell Keefer I need half-a-dozen men, ten men, to run down Conrad. *Now*, you stupid son of a bitch, not next week! Go, for Chris'sake!'

The targeted man flushed at the name-calling, but turned his wild-eyed mount and started back across the creek.

As Brodie reloaded, urging the others to start into the timber up on Catamount Hill, a voice called from the far side of the creek,

'What the hell's all that shootin'?'

Brodie felt goosebumps ripple over his body as he wrenched around in the saddle. Sheriff Brad Tyrell and a dirty-looking stranger were sitting their sweating horses there.

'The hell's goin' on, Chick?' Tyrell called impatiently. 'Sounded like a damn war in full swing!'

Brodie shook his head and walked his quivering mount into the creek, crossing slowly. He forced a welcoming smile.

'Hell, am I glad to see you, Brad! That damn sodbuster — Conrad! He's gone loco. Me and the boys noticed he'd grabbed some of our mavericks and we come over to brace him and — well, he was beatin' the hell outa that ranny he's had helpin' him with his cabin. Musta had a difficulty.'

He gestured to the prone and bloody form of Randy McLaren lying on the ground, half-concealed by a small bush. Ringo Magraw ripped out a curse, dismounted and ran to his battered pard.

'Conrad's gone loco?' asked a puzzled Tyrell.

'Somethin' musta goosed him. He tried to kill me, laid out Dog Beale, grabbed a rifle and had my men runnin' about like Injuns scatterin' from a cavalry charge. He's up yonder somewhere, on Catamount. I just sent Todd back to the ranch to get some more men.'

'Fine, but I'm here now and I'll take charge of any posse.'

'Sure, Brad, that's your right. Christ, I've never seen anyone go as loco as Conrad! He's dangerous, ready to kill — we're just lucky none of his shots hit . . . '

Ringo, face white and angry, Randy's head cradled in his lap looked up, calling, 'We need a sawbones here! Pronto! And I'm tellin' you now, Sheriff, you can keep your damn posse! I want this bastard for myself! Lookit he's done to Randy's hands!'

Brad Tyler, grim-faced, turned away from the unconscious figure of the battered and brutalized McLaren.

'Let's get organized. You ride with the posse or stay the hell out of it, Ringo. I don't want no vigilantes, understand? I want this sonuver behind bars by sundown!'

Brodie looked at his dishevelled, somewhat confused men. He spoke quietly out of the corner of his mouth.

'Notice he din' say he wanted Conrad alive. You boys can bet Keefer'll pay a bonus for makin' sure he's brought in dead — savvy?'

Money talks loud to a hardcase crew like these Slash K riders, and each and every one nodded, starting to reload their weapons.

* * *

Conrad was lucky.

Lucky to have gotten away when and how he did; lucky he had a good strong horse under him — a long-legged, big-chested buckskin with a cream patch above the tailbutt — and lucky because there was a rifle in the saddle scabbard. He found ammunition in the saddle-bags, too, a spare shirt that would likely fit, and grub in the warbag. He had still been wearing his own cartridge belt and empty holster — they had taken his Colt when they had jumped him — but the holster was no longer empty. The six-gun he had wrested from the Slash K rider now filled the leather. So he was primed and ready for bear, or those sons of bitches Brodie would send after him.

He wasn't a man who cared for killing other men — there had been too much of that during the War — but he knew he would never rest easy again until he had killed Chick Brodie. To call him an animal was to insult all animals. He had two counts against him: Charley Reece and now Randy.

If it turned out he was acting on Keefer's instructions, then Keefer would pay, too. No compromise.

But for now, he was a fugitive and had to concentrate on staying ahead of that damn posse he had seen from the ridge top.

Sunflash from one man's shirt warned him Sheriff Tyrell was there and he had watched the man break up the posse into three groups. Must be a dozen men down there and they all knew this country better than he did.

Given time, he could maybe lose them — temporarily, leastways — but he knew he wouldn't get that time. They were coming and coming fast.

Every one of them had stopped to reload both tifle and pistol, so he figured the order was 'Shoot to kill!'

God alone knew what kind of lies Brodie had told the law, but Conrad couldn't stay around to find out.

He wasn't going to run far. *He wanted Brodie.*

And if he had to risk his own neck to get the man, so be it.

Decision made, he turned the big buckskin and headed into the tangled wilderness of the Catamount Hills.

4

HUNTED

Keefer had been glad enough to provide a buckboard to carry the injured Randy into town. He had kept his face carefully blank when the man called Ringo had said Randy had been beaten by Russ Conrad. Keefer knew damn well that wasn't true: Brodie had gone there on his orders to haze Conrad to the limit, and beating-up on Randy was the perfect way to do it. It had worked, too: the man now had a posse under Brad Tyrell hunting him, which suited Keefer fine.

'I don't aim to let the sonuver get away with it,' Ringo told the rancher heavily, watching Keefer's face.

'Man must be loco,' he opined. 'He gunwhipped my ramrod and one of my men in town the first day he was here.

Setting the scene, you might say, for the way he aimed to run things. Well, Sheriff Tyrell will no doubt take care of him. Your friend looks in a bad way, Mr Magraw.'

Ringo had no argument with that and Keefer watched him drive the buckboard out of the yard, then turned to Todd as the man cleared his throat.

'Din' want to give this to you while Ringo was here.' He fumbled a worn, sweat-darkened wallet out of his shirt pocket and offered it to the rancher. 'Chick found this in Conrad's saddlebags.'

Keefer opened the wallet, saw a few low denomination bills there, and then took out a creased square of paper and unfolded it. He arched his eyebrows. 'Receipt from the bank for safe storage of 'legal papers', deposited by Conrad . . . ' He looked up at the puzzled Todd. 'I wonder just what legal papers they'd be?'

Todd shrugged beefy shoulders. Keefer read the paper again. 'This is Benjamin

Fallon's signature all right. Looks like I better ride to town. Saddle my black, Todd. Quickly!'

As the man hurried towards the corrals, Keefer tapped the refolded paper against his white teeth. If his hunch was right he'd have to put a little pressure on Fallon, but that shouldn't be hard. More than half the total money in the bank belonged to Keefer — Benjamin Fallon wouldn't want to risk losing his best client. He'd do as he was told.

★   ★   ★

Dog Beale was forced off the high cliff trail by Chick Brodie about mid-afternoon.

The climb had been dangerous right from the start, only about a foot-and-a-half of trail clinging to the mountain with an almost vertical drop on the open side. They were riding Indian file, Brodie behind Beale, when Chick swore, hauled rein, stood in the stirrups and pointed up-slope past Beale.

'There! By the thicket! Somethin' moved . . . Looked like Conrad's blue shirt!'

Dog Beale stood in his stirrups also and shaded his eyes. 'Where . . . ? Damned if I can see anythin'.'

'Keep movin'! Get up there before we lose him!'

Brodie, in his impatience, touched his spurs to his mount's flanks and startled it into a leap. It rammed the rump of Dog Beale's horse and the man let out a wild yell as the animal whinnied and swerved — and stepped off the trail.

Beale yelled as he felt himself going out into space. The horse fell away from under him. He still had a death-grip on the reins and they jerked his arms violently, before sending him into an uncontrolled tumble. Eyes big as hen's eggs, he fell away down the steep slope, starting to scream now, the horse upside down, legs flailing, whickering madly, saliva hanging in silver arcs above its jerking head.

Shocked, Brodie held his own mount in check, leaned forward over the arching neck to watch as first Beale's horse bounced and thudded and skidded down the steep mountainside, quickly followed by Dog himself.

The man jerked and bounced several times, somersaulting, limbs flailing, and then he hit on the back of his neck, slid and skidded into a pile of rocks where the broken body of the horse already lay, blood oozing over the shale.

Brodie swore. 'You OK, Dog?' he called foolishly. A blind man could see Beale was far from being 'OK', the way he was lying, legs twisted, blood on his face. 'Ah, shoot! What you wanta go an' do that for, damnit!'

Chick dismounted, took a look at the broken edge of the trail and cautiously leaned out to look down the slope. He shook his head. *He wasn't going down there! No, sir! Even if he could make it in one piece, there was no way back up a slope that steep. Not with a hurt man — or a dead one.*

He stepped back and gave a perfunctory salute. He frowned as one of

58

Beale's arms moved jerkily. Even from up here he could see it was broken, but he was surprised the man was still alive. He shrugged and mounted his horse again. Settling into leather he cocked his head slightly. Once he thought he had heard Dog Beale call his name.

'Sorry, Dog, I ain't comin' down. *Adios*. See you in hell when I get there!'

He looked up the trail to the thicket where he thought he had caught a glimpse of Conrad's shirt. He tensed as he saw the flash of blue again, then laughed shortly.

'Hell, only a bluejay flutterin' around its nest. How about that, Dog? A bird I could hold in one hand killed you! Now ain't that somethin'!'

Still chuckling, he rode up the trail very slowly.

⋆ ⋆ ⋆

Higher up on the same part of the mountain, Russ Conrad heard the panicked shrilling of Beale's horse. His ears judged by the sound that the animal was falling, the piercing whinnies fading slowly, yet echoing a little, too.

He had heard those sounds before, several times, in the army. He had been leading 24 Troop on a night ride over a place called the Devil's Rump in Colorado. The oldest trooper was no more than twenty-three, the rest greenhorns with most of them never having heard a shot fired in anger. Some had never even ridden a horse before the captain had given him the job of not only whipping them into shape, but doing it in three days, and then leading a night raid on the Union paddlewheelers loading up with supplies at the Eagle Bend of the Colorado River.

Before they had even come within sight of the river, three of the young recruits had gone off the trail and into Eternity. Each time, their mounts had made the same frantic cries as those he heard now.

He ought to have lifted his reins, jammed in his spurs and put the buckskin deeper into the timber. But he hesitated, because that night on the Devil's Rump, all those years ago, he had decided all three of his soldiers must have been killed in the fall. It wasn't until two weeks later that he learned two had survived the fall, one man dying later, the other recovering, but a cripple, one shattered leg having to be amputated. He had been the youngest of all the troopers — barely nineteen. His name was Willard Kennedy and his folks had spat on Conrad when he had gone to see them after the war had ended in some effort at atonement for his negligence. Once in a while, he still came jerking out of sleep, sweat chilling him, hearing those awful animal cries fading into the night . . .

'You're a damn fool!' he muttered, and set his horse away from the heavy timber, working back through the thicket towards the cliff trail.

Halting above it in a clump of huge, egg-shaped boulders, rifle-butt on his thigh, he carefully scanned the mountain-slope.

His hand tensed on the rifle as he saw a rider to his left, going away from him, down the easy slope of the range. Brodie! The rifle came swiftly to his shoulder and he felt the sun-warmed wood of the stock against his cheek, the cooler touch of the gunmetal of the trigger as his finger curled around it.

'I'll give you as much chance as you gave Randy McLaren, Brodie!'

His finger tightened as he drew careful bead and then he slacked off quickly as he heard Brad Tyrell's voice calling up the far slope to Brodie.

'What's happened up there, Chick? We heard a horse screamin'. You got a mountain cat there?'

'Nah,' Brodie answered immediately. 'Dog Beale: blamed fool, wasn't watchin' the trail, walked his mount clear off into space.'

A pause, then the sheriff's voice again. 'He dead?'

'As yes't'y's breakfast — seen sign of Conrad?'

'Lost him down in Dragonfly Draw

— He din' come over the hill here?'

'No. I'd've seen him.'

'You best come join my bunch and we can spread out after we make a plan. We're not goin' to run him down before dark by the looks of it.

'Long as we *do* run the sonuver down!'

Brodie dropped out of sight below the rise and Conrad let out a breath he hadn't realized he was holding, heard the posse riding back down the far side.

That was close. If he had shot at Brodie, he would have had half-a-dozen men coming at him.

He waited in the shade until he could see Tyrell's group far below on the flats. They were heading towards the draw where he had paused to cover his tracks and lay a false trail. *Dragonfly Draw*, he supposed. Then he scrubbed a hand down his stubbled jaw, pursed his lips and set his mount down the narrow, dangerous trail Brodie and Beale must have taken.

He wasn't sure that Dog Beale was

worth it, but something inside him urged him to check. There was an image of young Kennedy sitting right there before his eyes and it wouldn't go away . . .

Dog was alive but must be in tremendous pain, Conrad thought, as he examined the man after a difficult climb down the very steep slope. One leg broken, the ankle on the opposite leg shattered. A busted arm, some ribs, and a split in his scalp on the back of his head from which blood ran like a tap, face battered and gashed and scraped. Conrad had little to work with but tore up the spare shirt in the buckskin's saddle-bags, used canteen water to clean Beale's numerous wounds, cut sticks with his clasp knife and sliced Dog's own belt into several strands to use to tie them firmly around the broken leg by way of a splint. All he could do for the ankle was bind it tightly.

Dog moaned and groaned and swore and punched at him feebly, only half-conscious. Conrad forced some more water between his smashed lips. The man coughed and grimaced at the pain it caused him.

'Try not to cough. You could drive the splintered ends of the ribs into your lungs.'

Dog's eyes came into proper focus suddenly. He gave a start. 'Christ! It's you!' He looked down at himself. 'Wha — ? Why you helpin' . . . me?'

'I'd do the same for a real dog — Dog.'

'But . . . you . . . hell, Chick rode off an' . . . left me. He's s'posed to be my . . . friend . . . '

'You got Brodie for a friend, you won't need enemies. Dog, why the hell is that posse after me?'

'Chick told 'em was you beat-up McLaren.'

Conrad swore softly. 'Something else to square away!'

Beale was having trouble breathing. He couldn't take his staring eyes from Conrad. 'What . . . now?'

Conrad looked at the steep slope.

'Well, I don't think I can get you up there — you'd need someone up top helping.'

'Look!' Dog choked, trying to point with his splinted arm and grimacing in pain. 'C-cat!'

Conrad saw the cougar slinking through the brush at the edge of some rocks. The blood scent from the shattered carcass of the horse must be driving it wild for it to come in at ground level this way: they generally liked to be above their prey, with all the advantages that height gave. Conrad lifted the rifle, fired into the air, worked the lever again and fired a second time.

'Judas! Whyn't you shoot *at* it?'

Conrad wondered that himself. Maybe it was because he had been caught up in the mass slaughter of buffalo some years ago, sickened by the shocking waste of meat that could have fed a dozen tribes, the ground squelching with blood. He had been kind of — careful with wild things ever since, killed only what he could eat or use in some way.

He stood. 'Well, I'll be going, Dog.'

'Hey, don't! Don't leave me . . . that cat'll be back . . . '

'Not for a while. Tyrell ought to be here by then.' At Beale's frown, he added, 'He's got some men on the easy side of the range. He'll have heard the shooting.'

Conrad took Beale's six-gun from the man's holster. It was battered and dented from the fall but would fire. He left it where Dog could reach it with a little effort. 'You can drive him off again till they get here.'

'You knew scaring off that cat'd bring Tyrell?'

'Easiest way of getting someone here,' Conrad said. 'I'll be long gone by then.' He rammed his rifle through the back of his belt as he made ready to climb back up the steep slope to the trail above. 'Cat won't bother you if you get off a couple shots. *Adios*, Dog. You're not much of a man, but I hope you make it. You've got a chance now, anyway.'

Beale watched him go, fighting another wave of blackness that threatened to overwhelm him. He tried to lift the gun and draw a bead. 'You — come back here or I — I'll shoot!' he rasped.

Russ Conrad smiled, shook his head and started climbing up the slope.

Beale slumped, racked by massive pain.

★   ★   ★

Tyrell looked accusingly at Brodie as did some of the others in the group. 'You said he was dead!'

Chick Brodie shrugged, staring down at the bandaged and splinted Beale. 'Well, look at the drop. You figure a man'd be alive after that?'

'He was!'

'Looked dead to me. C'mon, let's get things movin' here. What we gonna do with Dog?'

Tyrell scratched at his head beneath his hat, watching the small group. He glanced at the sky, which was turning brassy now, shadows of the hills lengthening.

'Well, Conrad's done the first aid. I reckon we better get Dog back to town to the sawbones, then pick up fresh mounts and proper supplies, ready to come back here first thing in the mornin' and start a real search.'

That seemed to suit the others — except Brodie who scowled. 'We'll lose Conrad! He'll be halfway to Denver by then!'

'Reckon not — he don't know these hills.'

Brodie snorted. 'No — and look how he's outfoxed us all damn day!'

'He won't move much in the dark,' Tyrell insisted. 'We'll find him tomorrow for sure.' The sheriff nodded to the men. 'We'll build a travois. We ought to make town by sundown.'

'I'm takin' my men back to Slash K,' Brodie growled. 'We can get started earlier from there.'

'Suit yourself, but you wait at the Calico Bend for me to link up with my part of the posse.'

'Hell! More time wasted!'

Brad Tyrell's eyes narrowed. 'Not if it stops you and your crew playin' vigilante, Chick. Now that's it. I want Conrad taken alive, without any bullets in him. I mean it.'

He glared at Brodie and his men, but felt that he wasn't getting much back by way of respect, or obedience.

Brodie scowled but said no more.

5

MAN ALONE

All day, Conrad could recall the survey map pretty well, but once it was dark he wasn't sure of his bearings.

After climbing the cliff where he had left Dog, he had heard Tyrell and his men coming fast, reckless of the narrow trail. Dog, no doubt in a panic now shadows were deepening down in the hollow where he lay, triggered two shots from his six-gun, probably at the big cat sniffing around.

Conrad wheeled the buckskin into heavy timber and dismounted, standing beside it, hand over the horse's muzzle as Tyrell, Brodie and the others thundered by below him.

Once he heard them make shouting contact with Dog, he walked the buckskin out of the timber and started slowly across the slope, keeping to the shadowed side. He made it without being seen, then topped out on the ridge, paused long enough to look around so as to get some bearings and headed for another distant creek with dark, pocketed hills beyond.

It looked like the kind of country a man on the run might make for. It would have to do for tonight, anyway. In the morning he would climb as high as he could and hope to get his bearings once again.

He made cold camp and slept fitfully, with his Colt loose in the holster and his rifle beside him under the blanket.

Canteen water and jerky was his breakfast and a slim smoke in the saddle as he laboured up to the top of the ridge. It was steep and the horse was reluctant, balked several times. Conrad was sweating by the time he got to the top, waited for the sun to wash more brightly over the basin and then tried to recognize landmarks.

He was just figuring it out by the run

of the two creeks that joined below a bluff and became the single stream that flowed across the south-west corner of his land, when he saw movement on a bend.

He swore softly, instinctively pulling the buckskin back into the trees. That looked mighty like the posse forming up again down there, walking their mounts through the shallows, picking up more or less where they had left off yesterday.

Goddamnit! In terms of distance, all he had achieved was a couple of miles!

In this kind of country, it amounted to no more than a hop, step and a jump! Especially to men who knew what they were doing and where they were going.

Feeling tense now, he mounted and, holding the rifle in one hand, turned the buckskin, making deeper into the dark hills.

Totally strange country for him.

★   ★   ★

Ringo awoke, stiff and sore from sleeping in the chair on the small porch outside Doctor Moreno's infirmary.

He swung his arms and unkinked his back, spat over the rail and went in through the door. The doctor, olive skinned due to his ancestry, flashed his dark eyes at him as he stroked his pointed beard.

'I was just coming to see if you were awake.'

'How is he, Doc?' Ringo asked grimly and tensed when he saw the medic carefully compose his narrow face. 'Gimme it straight, Doc.'

Moreno nodded. 'As I suspected last night but did not tell you, your friend has a badly fractured skull and when — if — he regains consciousness, there is a good chance he may not remember anything — and I mean by that, not even his own name. His hands, of course, will take a long while to heal.'

Ringo Magraw went very still. 'He might be — what's the word, Doc? Teched? A dummy? Imbecile . . . ?'

Moreno placed a hand on the man's arm lightly. 'None of those terms are suitable, Mr Magraw! There may be brain damage. It's not inevitable, but his memory could be affected.'

'He is gonna make it OK then?'

'I think we should wait and see, my friend. He has had a bad — a *very* bad beating and he has a long, difficult fight ahead of him.'

'How long before he comes round?'

Moreno shook his head slowly. 'Mr Magraw, I can not say, but I suggest you find yourself some lodgings in town as it may be some days, even weeks before — '

Ringo's face was grim. 'Doc, I badly want to stay with Randy, but I can't do it. I can't wait around. I gotta be doin' somethin', and the best thing I can think of is ride with the posse that's tryin' to run down the son of a bitch who done this to Randy.'

Moreno studied the hard, blocky face and nodded gently. 'Come have some breakfast before you leave. My wife is preparing it now. Sheriff Tyrell rode back into town last night so you will find him down at his office later.'

Ringo hesitated, but finally nodded his thanks and went inside with the medico, who pointed to his left. At the same time there came a hacking, bubbling cough from the infirmary section and Ringo looked alarmed.

'Through there, Mr Magraw. Enjoy your breakfast. I have another dying patient I must attend to, besides your friend.'

*　*　*

Ali Tyrell set a platter of bacon and eggs before her brother, noting his red eyes and dull manner and other signs of lack of sleep. 'You need to rest more before going back to Catamount Hill, Brad.'

'Nope, Sis. That feller Conrad's been on the loose too long already. You seen what he done to Randy McLaren. He's a mighty *malo hombre*. I mean, a man who was helping him build his home!

To turn on him like that! For whatever reason!'

'I can't believe it of him, Brad. Oh, I know! You think I don't know him well enough to say that, but I . . . feel it. I sensed his innate decency.'

He smiled briefly, crookedly. 'Woman's intuition, huh?'

'I suppose so. Anyway, he showed some humanity by climbing down that dangerous cliff and doctoring Dog Beale, who, heaven knows, is not what you might call a good man. *That* is not the action of a *malo hombre*!'

Tyrell stopped chewing, looked at her, frowning. 'I know,' he said finally. 'Don't seem to make any sense, but there were plenty of witnesses who backed up Brodie's story.'

'As when Charley Reece was shot! All from Slash K!'

He sighed. 'Yeah, well, I've put it straight to Brodie that I want Conrad alive; I aim to get the truth of this, Ali.'

'How is Dog, anyway?'

'Pretty bad. Seems the jolting in the

travois helped tear up his lungs due to his broken ribs . . . ' He shook his head. 'I have to take the blame for that, I guess, hurryin' the men along the way I did.'

She dropped a hand to his shoulder. 'You did what you thought was best, Brad. Dog Beale would probably be dead already if you hadn't brought him in.'

'Yeah — Hell! Who's that this early?'

He swung around in his chair as there was a rap on the front door. Ali said, 'I'll go,' and, wiping her hands on her apron hurried through.

When she came back she was followed by Ringo Magraw. He nodded, holding his hat in one hand, his rifle in the other.

'Want to join your posse, Sher'ff.'

Brad finished a mouthful, washed it down with some coffee before answering. He looked pointedly at the rifle.

'All right, but I want this man caught alive and brought in for questioning. You got any other notions, you're not coming, that's flat, Ringo.'

Ringo, face deadpan, nodded. 'I'll abide by your rules, Sheriff.'

Ali looked at her brother's face and saw the uncertainty there, but he said, 'Good, go get your mount. We'll be pulling out in fifteen minutes.'

As Ringo hurried out, Ali said, worriedly, 'I think that man wants to kill Russ Conrad very, very badly!'

'I know he does, Sis. So does Chick Brodie. I'm gonna have a helluva job bringin' in Conrad alive.'

★   ★   ★

Brodie did not keep the rendezvous at Eagle Bend.

There wasn't even any fresh sign to show that he and his Slash K men had been there and gone again. The sheriff swore, pushed his hat back from his sweaty face as he looked up at the surrounding hills.

'Damn you, Chick!' he gritted. He knew what Brodie had done: gone straight after Conrad, headed up to the area they had quit last night. Angrily, Brad Tyrell turned to his posse, twelve men including Ringo Magraw.

'We'll break into three groups. Huck, you take one, you another, Mack, and the rest come with me — that includes you, Ringo.'

Magraw shook his head. 'I've been scoutin' for trail herds for over ten years, Sher'ff. Had three more before that in the army. Someone show me Conrad's tracks and I'll nail him before sundown.'

Tyrell narrowed his gaze. 'You will not nail him! I want him alive, I told you that and if — '

Ringo waved a hand irritably. 'I meant nail him down, locate him and pin him down till you bring up your men.'

Tyrell looked dubious. But he knew there wasn't a real tracker amongst his group, mostly townsmen. Brodie had good trackers from Slash K and the man himself was pretty damn sharp at trailing.

'Won't have to bring the men up, because we'll be right behind you.'

Ringo nodded. 'Once I see his sign, he's a goner.' Silently, he added, *You might be behind me for a while — but not after I see this bastard's tracks! I'll lose you like a dime fallin' through a hole in my pocket.*

*   ⋆   ⋆

They climbed up the narrow trail past where Dog Beale had gone over the edge and Tyrell showed Ringo tracks left by the big buckskin Conrad was now riding.

Without speaking, Ringo cast around and silently, walking, rifle in one hand, the other tugging on the reins of his horse, led the way back into timber above the trail. He stopped suddenly.

'God *damn*!' snapped Tyrell, whipping off his hat and almost throwing it on the ground in anger. 'The son of a bitch sat his hoss here and watched us ride in and go help Dog Beale! He must've been within fifty feet of us all the time!'

Ringo shook his head. 'He wouldn't hang around. Once you got workin' your way down that slope to where Beale was, Conrad took off. See? Headed up and over.'

A rider groaned. 'Straight into the Night-at-Noons! We'll never find him in there!'

'The *what*?' Ringo asked.

'Night-at-Noons,' Tyrell said tiredly. 'A tangle of hills with timber so thick it's almost permanent shadows. Someone said it's like night at noon in there and the name stuck . . . By hell, I'm wonderin' if Conrad knows this country better than we figure!'

'Well, them hills are hidin' a helluva lot of hardcases so they say,' said another posse man. 'If the law gets too close they can make it into Indian Territory in a day's ride.'

'Faster,' growled the sheriff. 'Those

owlhoots know all the shortcuts.'

'You think Conrad's makin' for the Territory?' Ringo Magraw asked.

Tyrell hesitated. 'He'd have to know the way. He claims he's never been here before. But he had a friend here, Charley Reece . . . coulda sent him a map.'

'Might've just run for cover in there because it looked so rugged,' opined the same townsman as before.

The sheriff started to answer when he stiffened. Ringo snapped his head up, too, and the posse men tensed in their saddles. Distant gunfire came rolling over the crest.

'Comin' from the Night-at-Noons!' someone said in hushed tones. 'I think I got business back in town.'

★　★　★

He didn't know how they had trapped him but they had somehow pinned him down on a ledge and there was just no place to go.

A minute before, he seemed to be a man alone, riding through these creepy, shadowed hills, the thick canopy of tree branches overhead even moaning in the breeze. He knew it was only high branches rubbing together and the sound amplified by the hollow trunks or those full of sap, but it made his mount uneasy. Having to constantly reassure the buckskin by word and actions had made *him* uneasy, too, irritable.

Conrad was recalling the survey map now but knew there had been no details of this area, just grey shading with the words 'Thick Tall Timber' printed over it. Someone had scrawled something in pencil, too, but he had been unable to make out all the words. Something about 'night' and 'noon'.

Anyway, he had ridden in here warily, figuring to check the place out. And he had found hoof marks! Only two or three, but taking a wide swing had showed him several others, too. Not all the same, which meant different horses, different riders.

So, thinking there might be other men in here who had a reason to hide, he started searching mighty cautiously. Anyone skulking in here likely had no use for strangers.

And that was what he thought: that the first shots were warnings from the denizens of these dark hills.

But he had broken through what turned out to be a much thinner screen of brush than he had allowed, into rocky country and he had found a rising trail to a bench with a rocky ledge. *That would give him a commanding view . . .*

Wrong! Well, no, it did give him a commanding view, but his ambushers had already figured out he would go to that ledge. And why not? It was the only place where he could get a good look at the thick timber and brush below.

But that also meant anyone waiting with a gun would have the place covered. And a half-dozen bullets raked the ledge, screaming from the rocks, laying grey streaks of lead across them, spraying shale dust and chips.

Conrad glimpsed smoke down at the brushline and put two fast shots into it. A man staggered back, a rifle falling from his hands, blood on his shoulder. He dropped from sight. More lead walked across his rock — from the side and above.

He rolled several times, landed on his back, rifle coming up. Hawk-like vision that had gotten him out of many a scrape in the past, spotted the small pall of powdersmoke drifting above two edge-to-edge egg-shaped rocks. His next three shots drummed out in a rapid beat, shearing hand-sized chips from the shale, raising dust, ramming away in hornet-like ricochets. Someone cursed and yelled, *'My eyes! I'm blinded!'*

He showed a portion of shirt and Conrad shot him, the man dropping out of sight without further sound. Spinning to his right, some sixth sense warning him, he felt stones pepper his shoulder through his worn shirt. There was a man up there, foolishly half-standing so as to get a better shot. It also gave Conrad a better shot and a single bullet brought the man tumbling down, arms and legs flailing.

A heavy volley from below made him squirm further back from the edge, but not before he glimpsed at least six Winchesters seeking to ventilate his lean body.

The man in the centre of the line was easily recognizable as Chick Brodie.

'Aw, for Chris'sake! How much lead is it gonna take to nail this son of a bitch! You idiots couldn't hit the side of a house!' Brodie roared.

Conrad could just make out Brodie now, crouching behind his own egg rock, thumbing shells into the loading gate. The fugitive took careful aim, triggered and grinned tightly as the rifle slammed from Brodie's grip, spinning out of sight behind him. Chick yelled and dived headlong for cover. A second shot from Conrad tore a heel off one of the man's riding boots.

'You get him, Chick?' one of the men called sarcastically, and earned himself an acid curse from the Slash K ramrod.

'We ain't gonna prise him outa there!' another man opined loudly. 'He's under that big black rock now.'

'Then shoot under it!' bawled Brodie, still shaken by Conrad's bullet wrenching the rifle from his hands.

Immediately, Conrad moved, kicking his way out from beneath the inward sloping rock, rolling across the ledge and falling into a shallow trench he hadn't seen before.

When the sounds of the wild, wasteful firing from below had dwindled, he heard Brodie throwing more curses at his men. But he couldn't see the ramrod. Still, it was time to scare these fools off.

Lifting his upper body warily, he thumbed six new shells into the magazine, levered one into the breech, and then sighted down the barrel. Men below were changing position, but none

88

of them could get higher than he was right now without being seen. Still, one man was stupid enough to try, squeezing into a narrow chimney between two tall boulders, writhing, and showing much of his body.

Conrad put his shot into the man's upper thigh or hip and the scream of agony made his blood turn cold. The man tumbled out and hit the rocks below, blood splashing.

It was all it took. Within minutes, Brodie and his men were fleeing down the slope, the recently wounded man left to drag himself under whatever cover he could find.

Conrad got to his feet, ran, crouching, to where his buckskin was sheltering and swung into saddle. He spurred away up the steep slope but only had a few yards of open rock to cover before he crashed into the shadowed brush and timber again.

They were still yelling behind him and he looked over his shoulder, grinning, slowing the mount.

When he turned to the front, there was a horseman sitting in the centre of the only way out, cradling a rifle that was pointing in Conrad's direction.

'And where the hell d'you think you're goin'?' the man asked harshly, lifting the weapon to his shoulder.

6

KIDD

The two posses met in the draw at the base of the range known as the Night-at-Noons.

Brodie and his crew were licking their wounds — they had four men down and one named Dally was somewhere back on the slope amongst the boulders below the ridge where Conrad had made his stand.

It was almost certain sure the man was dead.

No one volunteered to go back and check.

Brodie sat smoking on a small rock, shoulders slumped, his mind in turmoil. He figured he had had Conrad cold! Goddamn the man! He was a dead shot, knew how to use the country, actually *called the shots!*

He was still brooding when Brad Tyrell rode in with his posse, Ringo Magraw looking grim-faced as they hauled rein. The sheriff quit saddle before his mount had completely stopped, stood over Brodie who looked up slowly, face deadpan.

'You were s'posed to wait for me at the Eagle Bend!' snapped Tyrell, and his face darkened as Brodie shrugged.

'We left Slash K early — din' seem to make any sense to spend a hour or so coolin' our heels waitin' for you to arrive when we knew Conrad was headed into the Noons.'

'You knew, huh?' Tyrell snapped.

'Stood to reason. Only way left to him.'

'And you tracked him down? Caught him somewhere?'

Brodie moved a little uneasily. 'We-ell, we did glimpse him and kind of moved around, sendin' in a couple men he would be sure to spot.'

'In other words you drove him into an ambush!' Tyrell shook his head jerkily, mouth tight. 'By hell, Chick, if you killed him . . . !'

Brodie gave a harsh laugh, gestured to his men. 'Killed the son of a bitch? Look at what he done to us! And Wade Dally's back there somewhere, likely dead.'

'*Likely*, eh? You ride out and leave him the way you left Dog Beale?'

Brodie stood now, face craggy. 'Listen, anyone woulda figured Dog was dead after a fall like that!'

'Most men would've made sure. Don't you want to know how he is?'

Brodie shrugged, drew deeply on his cigarette. 'We're wastin' more time! Conrad'll be headed for the Injun territory we sit here all day chewin' the fat.'

'Dog's gonna die, Chicks. Lungs all tore up by his broken ribs.'

'Yeah . . . ? What about McLaren?'

'He likely won't make it, either. Fractured skull.'

'Well, he dies and Conrad's a murderer. He can be shot on sight. You hear that, boys?'

'Never mind!' roared Tyrell. 'I want him alive and the man who kills him except in self-defence is gonna see the inside of my jail till hell freezes over!'

The whole posse moved restlessly, but Brodie suddenly smiled crookedly. 'By the way, Mr Keefer's put up a three hundred dollar bounty on this Conrad — if anyone's interested.'

Tyrell cursed. A bounty like that to these men practically guaranteed that Russ Conrad would be brought in dead.

About this time he discovered Ringo was missing.

★   ★   ★

The man's name was Nathaniel Kidd and he lived in what appeared to be a dilapidated cabin on a rise, far back in the Night-at-Noons, screened by trees and heavy brush.

But there had been sight-paths cleared, branches trimmed, others stripped of leaves, brush pushed to one side so as to give a good view, and a line of fire, to the only approach from the basin below. The cabin may have looked like it was on its last legs from outside, but inside it had been prepared for a siege.

There were folding shelves beneath each window where spare ammunition could be laid out within easy reach. Eyeholes large enough to take a rifle barrel, with a small notch above cut for the sights. Heavy shutters made of hardwood planks held together by bolted iron straps, the log walls thick enough to stop any bullet. There were two heavy bars on the front door, one at head height, the other about the level of a man's knees.

The rear door was false and strong. Attackers could spend a lot of time trying to break it in before they found that out. Meantime, anyone in the cabin would have left by an exit that went *under* a side wall, the trap-door camouflaged by a stack of what looked like sacks of corn. But they were stuffed with sawdust and leaves, easily flung aside in a hurry. The exit came out in brush that had been cultivated almost up against the cabin wall.

'Good layout,' Conrad opined. 'Except for the brush.'

Kidd, a big man with the ugliest face Conrad had ever seen, looked at him hard. 'It's close so a man won't be seen comin' out.' One side of his face was a mass of twisted scar tissue and Conrad had seen enough burn wounds in the army to recognize this as being one — a bad one. Both Kidd's hands showed similar scars, too.

'Good for cover — unless someone sets it afire first. Then your cabin goes, too.'

Kidd gave a kind of jump. There was a hissing sound as he swore, thumped a fist down onto his leg. 'By Godfrey, you're right! How in *hell* I never figured that . . . Well, I been here a few years now and no one's ever found me.'

'Could come a time. All you need do is clean the brush back and dig a short tunnel from your wall. Shouldn't be too hard. Have it come inside the line of brush.'

Kidd studied him closely, poured another shot of moonshine into the clay cup in front of Conrad. His hand was shaking a little. Sweat rolled down his face.

Conrad had figured he was a dead man when he had first been confronted by Kidd with the loaded rifle: he'd thought he was a posse man. Then he'd cussed Conrad out, adding, 'Only thing stops me blowin' your head off is I don't want to bring Brodie and his crew back here.'

Conrad had smiled faintly. 'I think the sound of a gunshot might goose 'em even more. They're kinda jumpy.'

Kidd frowned, then nodded slowly, almost smiling. 'You did that to 'em, uh? Who are you?'

Conrad told him and was relieved to see the rifle hammer lowered although the barrel still pointed at him. 'So — Charley Reece mentioned you. Now I hear you kicked Keefer's ass and took that quarter-section offa him.'

'Not so much took, I just filed on it. He'd let it be known he'd put his brand on it for future use and it scared off a lot of folk. Guess I didn't know any better and filed on it.'

This time Kidd did laugh and gestured up the slope with his rifle. 'Ride on ahead and do just what I tell you.'

It had taken a long half-hour to make the climb up here to the cabin. Over coffee laced with tonsil-burning rotgut, Conrad said, 'You knew Charley, eh?'

'We were kinda friends. He had a rough deal from Keefer.'

'Keefer not a friend of yours?'

Kidd's eyes narrowed and he stared a long time in silence. Then he shook his head almost imperceptibly and touched dirty fingernails to his scarred face. 'I din' have an escape hole in the cabin I threw up on my quarter-section — one Keefer wanted, just north of where you tried to settle.'

'Still aim to. Keefer plays mighty rough, I guess.'

'You better believe it.'

'You have much to do with him now?'

Kidd laughed shortly. 'Askin' questions like that could get you killed.'

'You don't ask, you never learn anything.'

'Don't you know Tyrell wants you for beatin'-up on that feller was helpin' you?'

Conrad stiffened. 'So Dog Beale said. Was Brodie beat Randy to a pulp. He'd started on me, turned on Randy and was about to come back to me when I made a break. Wondered why it was a sheriff's posse and not just Keefer's crew coming after me.'

'They might take you in, but you'll be tied over your hoss. See you ain't too impressed. You want me to show you a way to the Injun Territory? Local law don't have no jurisdiction there. Has to be on a federal warrant.'

Conrad sipped some of his drink. 'No. Reckon I'll stay a while longer.

That land claim's in my name. Keefer can't do anything about that.'

'You get charged with beatin' a man to death, or nearly so, and they won't let you settle on no free land. Keefer's just makin' sure — likely he'll put out a bounty on you.'

'He put one on you?'

Kidd shrugged. 'Measly fifty bucks one time, but I ain't heard it's still there. You're a lot tougher than anyone figured, Conrad. You never learned shootin' like that in the army. Leastways, I never heard of anyone they taught that well.'

Conrad rolled a cigarette, offered the tobacco to Kidd who refused, took a chaw from a plug he kept in his pocket. Conrad lit up before answering.

'Grew up in a sod-roofed shack in Comanche country, down on the Pecos. Wiped us out one no-moon night. Just me and a dog got away. Found my way to some uncles up on the Red River and they raised me, taught me lots of things — '

'Includin' how to shoot, huh? And the Red — only a frog's leap from Badman's Territory, ain't it?'

Conrad smiled slowly. 'Asking questions like that could get a man killed.'

Kidd nodded, lifted a finger in acknowledgement. 'Yeah, well, I round-up a few mavericks to keep grub on the table, and I got me a ready market. Like I said, no one's found this place in years and I could do with some help — Keefer's got a lot more mavericks now than I can handle.'

His hard eyes bored into Conrad who seemed to be thinking it over. 'Some of these 'mavericks' wouldn't have a Slash K brand on their rumps, would they?'

Kidd spread his hands. 'Wouldn't be mavericks, then, would they? Not interested?'

'Wouldn't mind helping you out. But Brodie strikes me as a man who don't forgive or forget — Keefer, neither. They could make an extra effort to run me down. So they just might find your place when they're looking for me . . . your risk.'

Kidd thought about it, grinned suddenly and splashed moonshine into both their cups. 'Let's drink to that — I reckon the two of us could put that sonuver right outa business without even workin' up a sweat!'

Conrad picked up his cup. 'Yeah. I'll drink to that.'

* * *

Ringo Magraw didn't know the country any better than did Russ Conrad. But he was a man of the outdoors and wild trails and thought differently to town-bound men. Like Sheriff Tyrell: the man was a trier, seemed keen to live up to his badge, but he was restricted in his thinking. Had likely read up a book of rules and figured he couldn't go wrong by following them. Which was fine up to a point. But there were times when a man had to think for himself, make decisions that were outside any book.

So it was with Ringo. While the posse and Brodie's crew were arguing he looked into those deep-shadow hills they called, aptly enough he allowed, the Night-at-Noons. It was the logical place for a man on the run to make for. And Ringo was confident he could find Conrad's tracks if the fugitive was indeed in that area.

So he slipped quietly away while the others were growing more and more excited over the news that Fergus Keefer was offering $300 reward for Conrad's scalp. That's what it was, no matter how it was dressed up: 'Dead or Alive' invariably meant dead. It was less dangerous that way when there was a bounty to collect.

Conrad dying was OK by Ringo, but he wanted to be the one to do it. And he wanted to know why Conrad had turned on a man like Randy McLaren who had helped him throw up his cabin and was willing to spend more time building up the spread to prove-up requirements.

Ringo just couldn't figure how any man could do that and he wanted to know why it had happened.

Then he would gladly put a bullet in Conrad and ride out and not lose one second's sleep over the deed.

★   ★   ★

Ali Tyrell was surprised to see Fergus Keefer coming through the doorway of the Land Agency. He had never been in there before, always sent one of his men to do his business for him.

But one look at his face and she felt her heart lurch. Keefer was not known for his smiles, but the man was smiling now. He touched a hand lightly to his hatbrim.

'Miss Tyrell, can I take up a minute or two of your time?'

'I'm here to serve the public, Mr Keefer,' she replied formally and spread her hands. 'How can I help you?'

'Well, it's simple enough. I'd like to

file claim on that quarter-section at Two-way Creek.'

She sensed right away that there was more to this than met the eye. 'I'm afraid that's not possible. You know as well as I do that Russ Conrad has already filed on that land and is in the process of proving it up.'

Keefer's insincere smile widened. 'What I know is that this Mr Conrad is on the run, and that alone would make him ineligible to claim land given freely to settlers. So, while he may be throwing-up a cabin there, he's lost his right to legally settle in this basin.'

'You're wrong. He has already filed as required. I have a record of it here.' She brought out the ledger and leafed through, pointing to an entry. 'There — duly noted and dated.'

Keefer frowned. 'You have the claim form here?'

'No-o. Mr Conrad deposited it with the bank for safe-keeping. We usually encourage applicants to do that because this is only a small sub-agency that is not very secure. Anyone could break in without too much trouble.' She frowned, felt further misgivings as he looked puzzled, shook his head slowly. 'What's . . . wrong?'

'I've been to the bank on other business and Benjamin Fallon and I were discussing my planned expansion of Slash K. The Two-way Creek quarter-section came up but he said nothing about holding this Conrad's claim. In fact, we discussed financing my intention to build a small ranch on the section and put one of my men in to run it — sort of as a subsidiary to Slash K. I'm looking to develop my own breed of beef cattle and — '

Ali, heart racing, cut in, 'The quarter-section you're talking about is already filed on by Russell Conrad! I've just shown you the records.'

He craned his neck. 'Er — I don't see the actual papers.'

'I told you! We encourage the settlers to deposit their file papers with the bank! And I know Mr Conrad did this!

My official notification to Washington will be leaving with the next stage.'

Keefer smiled patiently. 'Well, I'm certainly willing to walk down to the bank now and ask Benjamin Fallon to once again check his records and settle this once and for all.'

'You've done something, haven't you?' Ali said, in a low voice, ignored his raised eyebrows and look of professed innocence. 'You've used your influence and — and power to get Banker Fallon to say he doesn't have Conrad's claim! I don't know what it can be but you've done something underhand.'

'Now look, Miss Tyrell, you just be careful! I've taken a good deal of innuendo from you, but I warn you, you make accusations you can't substantiate and you'll find yourself in a great deal of trouble. Legal trouble.'

She knew he was confident or he wouldn't smirk this way. She slammed the book closed and glared at him.

'If you'll wait until I get my wrap, I'll

walk with you to the bank.'

As she had feared, it was a waste of time. Benjamin Fallon had already made his deal with Keefer — whatever it was — and, sitting there smiling and sweating, flatly denied that Conrad had ever deposited the claim with him. A condescending discussion began and suddenly she was tired of it all, walked out in mid-sentence, leaving Keefer and Fallon blinking.

But once she was gone, they laughed, the banker saying, 'You better burn that original file claim, Fergus!'

★ ★ ★

Angrily, Ali walked through the town, up one side of Main and down the other. She paused outside the doctor's and went in, asking about both Randy McLaren and Dog Beale.

'McLaren still has a slight chance, I think,' the weary doctor told her quietly. 'He's not out of danger yet by a long way. They were very bad injuries.

But as for that cowhand . . . ' Moreno lifted his compassionate eyes to the woman's face. 'I'm afraid he died a short time ago.'

'Oh — well, he wasn't what you would call a *good* man, but I'm sorry he died that way — Brad will be upset. He blames himself for the broken ribs penetrating the lungs . . . '

'That may've hurried the process, but I don't think Dog Beale would have survived anyway.'

She nodded and started to turn away but Moreno's next words stopped her in her tracks.

'He did, however, show some decency just before the end.'

'I beg your pardon?'

'He may not have been what we usually think of as a good man but he was grateful to Russ Conrad for doing what he could for him at the base of that cliff. Or perhaps it was merely that he was resentful of the fact that Chick Brodie, a man he considered to be a friend, abandoned him in his time of need.'

'What're you saying, doctor?'

'Simply that Beale, with his last few breaths, told me that it was Brodie and not Conrad who beat Randy. Your brother's posse is hunting the wrong man, Miss Tyrell.'

7

WINNING HAND

Kidd knew these hills like he knew his own name. He said he had been waiting for a man who could and would stand up to Keefer for a long time. 'I'm gonna trust you, Conrad . . . and I better not be wrong!'

He led Conrad away from his cabin, down the slope and turned across it towards the west, angling downwards all the time. 'Might run into the posse down here, mightn't we?' Conrad asked, frowning slightly.

'If we do, it'll mean I've gone deaf and blind and lost my sense of smell.'

Conrad said no more, followed where Kidd led and they came out along a narrow stream by mid-morning. While the horses drank and they rolled cigarettes, Kidd said, 'Wonderin' what's goin' on?'

'Well, I can't read your mind.'

Kidd grinned briefly. 'Edgy, huh? You're OK here. Don't worry about it. Want to show you a canyon where I keep some of them mavericks that wander into my lariat noose.'

'Yeah — they can be careless critters, I've heard.'

'A *lot* of careless critters in this neck of the woods. You bothered by throwin' a wide loop?'

'Not if it lands on some of Slash K's cows.'

'Good. I've got me a feller who has a back run into Colorado. He's got some settlers there lined up and their pockets are draggin' with silver. They're lookin' for a short cut to buildin' up their herds with minimum layout.' They lit the cigarettes and, exhaling as he spoke, Kidd added, 'I been wonderin' how I can supply all he wants . . .'

He let it hang. 'Me?' Conrad asked.

'Help me grab some mavericks and drive 'em to my agent, and I'll keep you hid. You can earn a little *dinero* till you're ready to bust out.'

'What gave you the notion I'm gonna bust out?'

Kidd laughed. 'Man like you? Settin' back and lettin' a couple snakes like Brodie and Keefer frame you? Never happen, *amigo*. I know your kind . . . and I know this country. Lend me a hand and I'll help you when you're ready. I got no love for Keefer, or anyone works for him.'

He touched his scarred face and Conrad had the sense that it was automatic, that Kidd likely didn't even realize he was doing it. Just association: *Keefer — scars* . . .

'Sounds fair, but what happens to my land meantime?'

Kidd shook his head. 'Got no control over that.'

'Uh-huh. Well, are we on the way to round-up some of these careless mavericks now, or does that come later?'

'Mebbe tonight. Just wanted to show you where we'll be stashin' 'em, let you see the lay of the land. Now let's get outa here. Don't want anyone to see me this side of the mountain or they'll start wonderin'.'

They rode on down into the deep shadow of the hollow between the mountains and Kidd suddenly hauled rein, throwing a hand up in the halt sign. He leaned forward over his horse's head, looking past or through some brush that screened Conrad's view of what lay beyond. Kidd turned slowly, a tight grin stretching his lips. He slid his rifle from the scabbard, gestured ahead and then abruptly spurred forward, crashing his mount through the brush. Conrad, still not able to see what Kidd had seen, slid his six-gun into his hand and followed.

He almost hauled rein in his surprise. Chick Brodie was stretched full length beside his mount, drinking from a waterhole. He rolled swiftly on his back as he heard Kidd crash through the brush, reaching for the rifle on the ground beside him. Conrad spurred his mount around Kidd and rammed the horse into Brodie, the impact hurling the man into the waterhole. He lost his rifle, floundered and splashed, straightened, then lifted his hands slowly as the two men covered him.

'Someone's lucky day,' allowed Kidd. 'But I don't think it's yours, Chick.'

Brodie had eyes only for Conrad: he knew his main enemy here.

'Get outa there,' Conrad said quietly. Brodie hesitated and Conrad splashed his mount out into the water and the Slash K ramrod started for the bank swiftly. Just for the hell of it, Conrad allowed his big buckskin to nudge hard enough to knock Brodie off his feet. Gagging and spitting, the ramrod stumbled out on to the bank, water streaming from him. He turned as he straightened, looking up with something more than just wariness in his face now.

Conrad kicked him in the head, knocking him sprawling, then holstered his Colt and cleared leather in a leap that took him right up against the groggy ramrod. Conrad twisted fingers in Brodie's wet hair, yanked his head up and hit him squarely on the nose.

Sitting his horse, still holding the rifle, Kidd winced as he heard the cartilage crunch. Blood spurted and Brodie went down to one knee, a hand groping for support on the ground. Conrad kicked the man in the ribs and Brodie grunted as he fell sideways, crawling away painfully, a hand against his throbbing side. 'Learnt that from you, Chick!' Conrad gritted. He stalked and stood over Brodie as the man rolled on to his back, an arm across his head.

'Gimme a . . . chance you son of a . . . bitch!' he gasped.

'I'm giving you as much as you gave Randy McLaren.' Conrad kicked him again and again in the body, the blows rolling Brodie over the grass. 'And me.'

He stood back and let Brodie climb groggily to his feet, swaying, spitting blood. But the wariness had gone now. His face was contorted with hate and the urge to maim, even kill, his tormentor. With a gurgling yell, Chick lunged suddenly and Conrad stepped aside. But the grass was wet from Brodie and he slipped, almost lost balance. It was enough for Brodie to change direction and grab a handful of shirt.

He pulled Conrad violently towards him, not giving the man a chance to get his feet under him. A fist like a club took Russ on the side of the head and his boots left the ground, the shirt fabric ripping, tearing free of Brodie's grip. Conrad went down and badly wanted to stay there, head ringing, eyes rolling in their sockets, every tooth in his head feeling as if it had been drawn by pliers. He tasted blood and started to push up, making a massive effort to fight the nausea and dizziness that gripped him.

Brodie's boot took him low down on the ribcage, spilling him yards away. He slithered over the wet grass and Kidd frowned, showing his first sign of concern as Conrad lay there, blinking, hurt.

Get movin', feller! He'll stomp you!

Brodie threw Kidd a wary glance, but Kidd made no move to step in. Chick smiled faintly, nodded, and moved to close with Conrad. The man saw the Slash K man coming through a haze, rolled instinctively, bounced halfway to his feet this time. Brodie's heavy body hurtled into him and knocked him down and then big boots were stomping at his head and arms, belly, knees, keeping him moving frantically. Some of the kicks landed and shook Conrad badly. He slithered and rolled, felt a slamming pain between his shoulders as if hit by a flung rock. His head jerked on his neck and he spun around, bringing both legs up in an instinctive, lightning-fast move. Brodie ran on to the boots and grunted as he stopped dead, clawed a handful of air in an effort to keep balance. Conrad drew back his right leg, drove the boot into Brodie's bloody face and the man was hurled back, arms wide.

Moving more slowly than he would

have wished, Conrad staggered after the ramrod, caught him down on one knee. He ran the last few steps, lifted a leg into Brodie's chest and face. The man flew backwards, landed beside the pool again. Conrad dropped on to the man's back, grabbed his hair and jaw and thrust his face under the water. Brodie struggled and flailed and kicked and heaved, wrenching his head free for a moment and dragging as much water as air down into his straining lungs. He choked, thrashing.

It frightened him, not getting a full measure of air, and desperation made him arch his back like a snorting, buck-jumping bronco. Conrad slid off to one side, lunged back to renew his grip. But Brodie, gagging and vomiting water now in his efforts to gulp down some air, had enough reaction left to scoop up a handful of mud and hurl it into Conrad's face.

Half-blinded, by the time he had clawed mud out of his eyes, Conrad saw that Brodie was on his feet and coming in like a hunched buffalo ready to kill. He could barely lift his aching, throbbing arms, and he jumped back wildly, staggered, but managed to retain his balance.

He set his boots as Brodie reached him, ducked the first blow, feeling iron-hard knuckles rip across his scalp, searing his skull. But he ignored the fierce pain, batted aside the following hook and straight-armed Brodie. He turned his fist as it landed on the foreman's squashed nose and Brodie roared, rearing up in savage pain. He had both fists raised and clubbed them down now, aiming either side of Conrad's head.

Russ twisted, pulled his chin down on his chest, felt one blow thud on his shoulder where it joined his neck. The impact buckled one leg and from down low, he brought up his right, burying it deep into the arch beneath Brodie's ribs. The man stopped dead, gagging and choking. Conrad's other fist came up in a whistling uppercut that almost tore Brodie's head from his shoulders.

He dropped so fast that he fell across Conrad's bent leg and pinned him briefly. Conrad kicked free and made three attempts before he was able to stand erect. Brodie's arms windmilled one final time as he flopped on to his bloody face.

Water and blood and mud streamed from Conrad. He looked like he was squinting but that was only because his left eye was rapidly closing. Blood dribbled from a split lip, ran over a torn eyebrow, oozed from throbbing nostrils. His knuckles were split and his hands looked raw. They would be swollen and painful and awkward later, he knew.

But for all that, he was the winner and looked a whole damn sight better than the broken figure of Chick Brodie who had one leg and arm now dangling into the waterhole.

'I ain't never gonna get you mad at me,' Kidd opined. 'Whyn't you just push him in and let him drown? Chick won't be no loss.'

Conrad shook his head, but it seemed a long time before he was able to speak some intelligible words. 'Want him . . . to tell . . . sheriff . . . I din' beat Randy . . . '

Kidd shrugged. 'That's OK, but me — I'd kill the snake. I can hide you out in these hills forever.'

Conrad did squint up at him now. 'That ain't in my . . . plans, Kidd.'

'OK. Wash up and we'll go find some shade. I'll dab some iodine on the worst of them cuts and brew some coffee. Brodie might've come round by then.'

That sounded like a good idea to Conrad. Especially the coffee and iodine.

But it wasn't a pleasant experience just the same.

One side of his jaw ached and hurt like a stab with a knife blade when he tried to chew on a crumbly stale soda dodger. He reared back, smothering an involuntary curse, held the swollen jaw, face twisted in a grimace. 'I think he bust my jaw.'

'Wouldn't be flappin' it like that if it was. Lemme take a look.'

Kidd knelt in front of Conrad and made him turn his head. It was hard to make out the original lines of the man's face, there was so much swelling and a nest of bruises that looked like some kid's pastel colouring of a map of a foreign country. He tried to prise the battered mouth open.

'Judas priest!' Conrad groaned, shoving Kidd away as the man probed and squeezed. 'Hell almighty, anyone ever tell you you got a touch like a damn grizzly scratching a bee sting?'

'No, but a fat, cow-eyed gal once told me I had a velvet touch. 'Course she was kinda insulated by three, four inches of flab . . . See if you can open your mouth wider.'

'Damn! But it . . . *hurts*!'

'I believe it!' Kidd sat back, frowning. 'I think you got a broken tooth in there stickin' in the jaw hinge. I can likely yank it. Got a pair of pliers in my saddle-bags.'

'And they can damn well stay there! You ain't poking around in my mouth — *Aw, Christ*!'

Kidd spread his big hands. 'Up to you, but we only got jerky for grub and even if I shot a deer and gave you a piece of its liver, I reckon it'd hurt like a hot corkscrew, a'twistin' and gougin' away in there on the jaw hinge, like scrapin' bone an' swellin' so you could hardly — '

'*All right! All right!*' Conrad was breathing fast now. 'You just go easy. I'm gonna hold a cocked six-gun in your brisket and you start yanking and twisting too damn hard, you're gonna be a dead man!'

Kidd shook his head slowly. 'Ah, pain, pain — makes a man forget who his real friends are — just when he needs 'em most.' He took a pair of rust-scaled long-nosed fencing pliers from his bag, snapped the jaws several times.

'You sterilize those things in hot water first!'

'Fire's a'dyin'. Don't want to risk lightin' another. Posse might spot it. Coffee pot's still hot though . . . '

He glanced through the bushes downslope to the waterhole where Brodie still lay, bloody and breathing stertorily, then dipped the pliers in the battered coffee pot. Conrad watched his every move, his belly knotted-up the way it did whenever he had to go to a dentist. But he steeled himself: if Kidd was right a piece of broken tooth was in there and if it became infected . . . 'Get it done, damn you!'

It took twelve agonizing minutes to remove the piece of broken molar, but Conrad later swore it wasn't less than a couple of hours. Kidd had to cut the mouth lining a little to reach the embedded piece of tooth. Then there was some awful twisting and turning and crunching of the pliers and Conrad eternally damned himself by taking the name of the Lord in vain so many times and in so many different ways.

But finally it was free and he could

move his jaw a lot less painfully. He spat some blood, rinsed his mouth with coffee, which he complained tasted of rust from the pliers.

'Iron's s'posed to be good for you,' Kidd told him, pleased with his handiwork. 'I've yanked hosses' teeth plenty times, but this's first one I ever done on a man.'

'It'll be the last on me! You enjoyed every minute of it, you goddamn sadist!'

'Ain't that what an artist is s'posed to do? Enjoy his work? Lotsa times some ungrateful folk don't appreciate his efforts and — ' Suddenly, Kidd frowned. 'You smell smoke?'

Conrad knew he didn't mean the wisps from the small camp-fire that was now no more than a pile of glowing coals. No, this was real brushfire smoke Kidd was talking about . . . and the smell was strong. Conrad sat up straighter.

Kidd leapt to his feet, looking around wildly, yelling, 'Hell's teeth!'

A roaring sound hammered across the slope as a wall of flames suddenly leapt high and swept towards them through the dry brush, driven by the hot wind that had sprung up.

At the same instant, Conrad and Kidd both looked down sharply towards the waterhole.

There was no sign of Chick Brodie. Only blood stains on the churned grass where he had lain, and these were fast fading from sight as the heavy smoke rolled in, blurring the entire area, stinging eyes and throats.

Conrad spat blood, holding his throbbing jaw.

They had given too much attention to that and not enough to Brodie. Now, it looked as though the Slash K ramrod had found himself a winning hand after all.

A *hot* hand.

8

TRIAL BY FIRE

Ali Tyrell was lost. It didn't surprise her. While she liked to take a Sunday afternoon ride in the buggy she had bought some time ago, following the creek to its junction with the other stream where the grass was lush and green and the creek fork made a series of small waterfalls, she knew little of the country beyond that point.

She had been into the ranges with Brad and a couple of would-be beaux but only to the nearest draws and sandy bends in the stream. Picnic places where there were shady trees and wildflowers and birdsong. Like most other folk, she had always avoided the dark, shadowed area known as the Night-at-Noons, made uncomfortable by the lurid tales of wild men living in there just waiting to pounce and ravish any unwary woman fool enough to ride within their reach. But she had heard Brad when he had gathered his small posse, telling the men that he was convinced Russ Conrad would make for those hills.

'He don't know 'em any better'n we do,' one man had called. 'Likely a sight less!'

Brad acknowledged this, countering with, 'He doesn't know any of the country around here any better than we do. Sure, he might know his quarter-section but he's been too blamed busy workin' it till now to get to know anywhere else. So, bein' the smart *hombre* I figure him for, he'll make for the wildest neck of the woods he can find and try to lose himself there: which means the Night-at-Noons.'

It seemed to make sense and although they growled at the thought of spending time in the Noons, the posse accepted it and they left town at the gallop.

Ali, after learning about Dog Beale's deathbed confession, knew she had to get to Brad and tell him that Conrad was innocent of beating poor Randy McLaren to a pulp. Conrad was not the type of man who would maim anyone the way Randy had been, no matter what the provocation. But she could readily believe it of Chick Brodie. So she had to reach Brad, have him call off the posse before Conrad was captured and harmed: or, worse, *killed*, seeing as Keefer had so obligingly put up a $300 bounty. *Three hundred dollars!* To dirt-poor men in a weatherbeaten north Texas town like Conifer Bend, it was a small fortune. Her stomach knotted at the thought that any of those men in the posse would probably shoot first and talk afterwards if Conrad was sighted . . .

She had started out full of enthusiasm and confidence, but she had not ventured fifteen minutes into the chill shadows of the Noons before she knew she just might have bitten off more than she could chew.

She was carrying a small .36 calibre Colt Navy revolver that had once belonged to her father during his early, town-taming days. It was an old black-powder model that had been drilled and reamed in its conversion to take rimfire cartridges. Her hand unconsciously dropped to the butt as she paused by a waterhole and allowed her grey mount to drink. She looked around, aware of cicadas humming loudly, strange rustles in the heavy brush and trees although there didn't seem to be any breeze down here. Brad had spoken of a place called Dogleg Draw and she had looked for it on a map before leaving. While there was no such place labelled, she did find something that could be it, going by its shape and the fact that it was not far into the dark ranges.

'We'll make it our rendezvous,' Brad had told his assembled men. 'Separate into twos and threes when we get there and come back to the draw by sundown

— unless we run Conrad to earth before that. We'll make camp there for the night, OK?'

She had thought she was on the right trail to the place she had seen on the map and which configured to a dogleg-like draw, but she couldn't find it. She knew she was foolish not to have brought the map with her, such as it was, even though there was little detail, but it would have been better than nothing.

She felt the first touches of fear rising within her and determinedly put them down. If there were wild men living here, on the fringes of the law or even outside it, surely they would run for cover, head deeper into the hills, once they knew posses were scouring the Noons . . .

Ali convinced herself that this was the correct logic and decided she would put *that* fear aside. But there was the basic, sweaty fear that came with the thought of simply being lost. No one was happy with not knowing where they were, especially in a wild, strange place. It was human nature to retreat from such a situation, and panic was always close to the surface.

But she was a strong person and although her flesh prickled with goose-bumps at the rustlings and distant coughing sounds — she thought, with genuine fear, that *that* must be a mountain lion — Ali searched the ground for tracks.

Not that she was an experienced tracker, of course, but she knew Brad had been complaining that his horse's right forefoot shoe had chipped a point on the previous manhunt in the other part of the hills. He hadn't had time for the smithy to replace the shoe, so she figured it would make a distinctive track in the soft earth and humus.

She almost cheered when she found a series of such marks, mixed with other more conventional tracks, followed them into timber — then abruptly lost them amongst a thick carpet of moist, dead leaves. Breathing hard, heart pounding, she turned the grey this way and that until, finally, the animal refused to answer her commands and crashed a path through brush that brought her out to the base of a slope where the sun, such as it was, still shone. It seemed to be overcast and yet it had been a cloudless day earlier.

She realized then that the light here was dulled by rolling clouds of thick smoke and that she had been smelling and tasting it for minutes now. Alarmed, she turned swiftly in the saddle, saw a wall of fire racing towards her through the brush, the sap sizzling and exploding like fire crackers. Flames writhed and danced across the tops of the brush as the fire created its own wind eddies and within moments she was surrounded by pulsing heat and licking flames.

The horse snorted, stamping, backing off this way, whirling left, then right, eyes rolling. It started to rear but she managed to talk quietly to it, patting the tossing head, barely able to form the words because of her heart pounding high in her throat. Smoke rasped and stung her eyes. She fumbled off her silk neckerchief, drew it up over her nose and mouth, knotting it quickly under her hair at the back.

There was no way out that she could see. There was a gleam of water ahead, maybe a small waterhole, but perhaps it was a creek she could plunge into and let the fire pass over her or burn its way around the banks.

The grey didn't want to move, snorting, close to panic, but she raked with the spurs, slapped with the rein ends, leaned over the tossing head, urging it on. At last, seemingly just as the flames actually seared the animal's rump, the grey leapt forward. She crouched low along its back, guiding it towards where she had seen the glint of water — she hoped that's what it was, anyway.

Yes! There it was! A small waterhole maybe seven or eight feet across . . . She felt her heart sink. It couldn't be very deep and certainly wasn't wide enough to give much protection from the fire. Perhaps she could dismount and lie down in the middle, submerge when the flames became too intense. But what about the grey . . . ?

As she hauled rein, the water up to the grey's underbelly, she looked around wildly for somewhere that would offer more safety. The fire was roaring, the terrifying sound filling her head. She could hear nothing but the hiss and crackling and storming of the flames; see nothing clearly, for the smoke blinded her, but she thought there was movement up the slope. No, it couldn't be, not that high up, although an eddy of wind had torn a peephole in the curtain of smoke briefly. But it closed again all too quickly before she could be certain she had seen riders or just one man — or nothing at all.

Decide, you little fool! a voice screamed in her head. There was no choice, now. Her skin was blistering, her clothes hot and beginning to smoulder. She dismounted, slapped the grey across the rump, then plunged into the muddy water, letting her body sink into its coolness. Coolness, that is, in comparison to the heated air above but she had already seen the steam rising from the edges.

My God! I could be boiled alive!

The grey, now free of her weight and control, whirled and ran out of the water, whinnying wildly as it disappeared into the smoke. She gave a choked cry and made a futile gesture after it.

Then flames writhed across the pool and, alarmed, she gulped a lungful of air, plunged her entire body under, fingers clawing into the mud and rocks of the bottom, the entire surface of the pool above disappearing beneath the writhing blanket of fire.

★　★　★

Conrad and Nathaniel Kidd had no choice, either: the firestorm was sweeping up the slope with the speed of a mustang stampede and they had to run before it.

There was thick timber above them and once in there it would be sheer hell trying to weave and dodge and control their mounts as they fought frantically to find a way out. And if the fire reached it, there would be no way out at all.

Once the fire took hold it would race ahead of them through the upper foliage, riding its own hellish wind, pinning them under an umbrella of flames and exploding, falling tree tops.

Kidd roared something, motioning ahead, skirting the lower edge of the stand of trees, indicating that Conrad should follow. Russ didn't hesitate: this was Kidd's stamping-ground and he would have to follow or go it alone, taking a risk that was almost certainly stupid — and could be fatal. He spurred the nervous buckskin after the rustler, was surprised when the man angled down towards the roaring sea of fire speeding up the slope.

Coughing, half blinded, the jarring of the horse setting his jaw throbbing like drums at a Comanche pow-wow, Conrad followed. He had to fight the buckskin who was rolling its eyes now in fear, the tossing head catching him a glancing blow and almost sweeping him out of the saddle. Stinging tears blurred his vision even more and he just glimpsed Kidd skidding his mount into one edge of the timber that seemed to butt up against a sheer rockface rising out of nowhere behind. The man disappeared in a moment.

The buckskin stumbling under him, still fighting the reins, Conrad made the same skidding turn and saw a dark maw opening up in front of him like the jaws of some monster waiting to devour both him and mount. He hauled rein instinctively.

The clatter of hoofs on stones drummed and echoed around the arched roof and broken walls of a big cave. He reined back as his eyes grew used to the abrupt change in light. The buckskin's propping forelegs skidded and the shoes screeched over rock as the animal stumbled and came to a halt with a shudder and a deep, growling snort of protest.

But the air, although smoky, was cooler in here, felt like a cold envelope surrounding their over-heated bodies. Squinting and using one hand to wipe tears and soot from his eyes, Conrad stared at Kidd who was dismounting, holding his horse's bridle as he spoke quietly to it. After a few calming words he glanced up at Conrad.

'Get off so he knows we're stayin'. He's had so many different commands in the last ten minutes he don't know whether he's a stallion or a steer.'

Conrad slid from the saddle, grimaced involuntarily at the jar that went through his body, and grabbed at his swollen jaw. Kidd couldn't help but notice.

'If that's all that bothers you, count yourself lucky.'

'I wish you the same kinda luck!'

Conrad gritted and Kidd grinned.

'It'll get better. We'll be OK in here. Might get a mouthful or two of smoke but there's a crack in the roof yonder. Any smoke'll be sucked out there.'

Looking around, Russ shook his head slowly. 'Just as well you knew of this place.'

'Wasn't gonna show it to you yet.' Kidd's grin widened at the way Conrad's head snapped up. 'Hey, I don't give away all my secrets in one bundle — same as you.'

'Fair enough. Pretty big cave . . . I see dried cow pats underfoot?'

'You don't miss much. Yeah, coupla times, Brodie or his men've come after me when I've been movin' some mavericks. Lost 'em both times by drivin' the cows in here. See in the corner? Hay — I keep renewin' it and chasin' the packrats outa the old stuff. Just in case.'

The mounts had discovered the hay and were much calmer now they had something to chew on. Beyond the entrance, screened partially by brush and tangled trees, they could see — and hear — the fire still roaring across the slope.

'Bad mistake, forgetting about Brodie like that,' Conrad said quietly, mopping his face gently.

'You had plenty to think about with that broken tooth in your jaw. If anyone should've kept tabs on him, was me . . . Still, the sonuver pulled a smart one, all right. Smoke'll bring the posse so we'll have to get outa here pronto as soon as the fire dies down.'

'There a back way out?'

'Not really. A man on foot could likely get through some of the crevices, but no hoss could do it.'

'Then I guess we sit and wait.' Conrad squatted and started to roll a cigarette. 'What I wouldn't give for a mouthful of rotgut pain-killer right now!' He touched his swollen face gently. 'Why don't we go have a look at the crevices you were talkin' about? It'll take my mind off the pain, maybe, and there's nothing else we can do right now.'

Conrad stood, newly made cigarette in his mouth, then said, 'Horses shouldn't wander off . . . '

'Nah. Not while that fire's goin'. Smoke won't worry 'em too much. C'mon. I'll get some hay to burn and show us the way . . . '

It might have taken Conrad's mind off the pain of his jaw but it was rugged going. The way was cramped and broken underfoot. Bats were thick on the walls despite the smoke and exploded into their faces about twenty yards in from the main cave. Conrad fell twice and hurt his already hurt ribs. Kidd helped him over an unusually broken patch. They must have been walking for ten minutes and the crevice by now was narrowing fast. Kidd held up the last handful of the burning hay on the end of his forked stick.

He pointed to the steep-angled slope. 'There's a hole a man can crawl through if he can suck his gut in a little.

Feel the up-draught? A little wider and I'd be able to push some cows through here. Be a mighty good short-cut.'

Conrad nodded, breathing hard. He hurt all over but studied the slope up to the hole and sat down again. 'Used to be on a demolition team in the army — learnt a deal about explosives. Reckon a few sticks of dynamite in the right place'd open this up, and your exit, too.'

Kidd snapped his head up. 'It's possible? I mean, hell! If I had this way open, it'd save me havin' to drive all round the mountain where I'm likely to get spotted by Slash K riders!'

'Yeah, reckon I could do it. Not easy, but it could be done in two or three sections. Lot of rubble to clear.'

Kidd grinned. 'Hey, you just earned your keep! I know where I can get my hands on some dynamite.'

Conrad nodded, sweating, his jaw-ache going down his neck into his upper chest now. 'We start back?'

'Sure. Man, I can't stop thinkin' of the possibilities if we can clear this passage!

I'll make a pile.'

It was easier going back and when they reached the main cave they could tell the fire had passed by or died out. The endless roaring of the flames had gone. Smoke hung in the cave in tendrils now, no longer swirling. Beyond the arched entrance lay a blackened, smouldering landscape. Then Kidd cursed aloud.

'The mounts've gone!' he snapped, and rushed past Conrad and out of the cave mouth.

Following slowly and awkwardly, Conrad straightened and stopped dead as he looked out into the dull daylight beyond the entrance. Kidd was standing there with his hands raised shoulder-high. Conrad crouched as several armed horsemen came into view, and he recognized Sheriff Brad Tyrell beneath the grime as the man said curtly, holding a cocked six-gun on Kidd, 'Where's Conrad? I want to see him — *now*!'

9

CAPTURE

Conrad hesitated. They hadn't seen him yet, back in the dark shadow of the cave, but where was there to run? Through the narrow crevice and then climb up to the small manhole that came out who-knew-where?

Yes! He answered himself. It was the only way out. And before the thought had properly formed in his head he was moving back across the cave into the solid darkness, groping his way into the crevice.

It was narrow enough and far enough back not to be noticed by any casual visitor: Kidd had had to point it out to Conrad earlier from inside the cave. He tried not to make any noise and thought likely he hadn't been heard because the horses outside were stomping in the still-hot ash of the slope and Kidd was talking fast and loud, holding the posse's attention, his voice covering any sounds he might be making.

The rustler was smart enough to know Conrad would take his chances in the crevice.

Kidd was certainly putting on an act. Yelling and gesticulating as he shouted at the posse.

'Where the hell were you when you were needed? Goddamnit, I was nearly burned alive by that fire! Dunno what's happened to Conrad. He just disappeared into the smoke. I was lucky enough to find this cave but I couldn't get out again to see if Conrad was following.'

'*Kidd*!' bawled Brad Tyrell suddenly. 'Will you for Chris'sakes shut up! We found your horse and that buckskin Conrad was riding, cowering in some rocks.'

'Just because the mounts were together don't mean the riders were, too,' interrupted Kidd, ignoring the thunderous look that crossed the sheriff's face.

'You just admitted Conrad was with you earlier!'

Figuring the posse had likely found the two sets of tracks side by side, the buckskin's and Kidd's own mount, the rustler said, 'Well, yeah for a while. We managed to jump Chick Brodie way down there at that waterhole, but he got the drop on us and we lost him. Think he started the fire.'

'Got the drop on you?' The sheriff looked cynical — he had now been diverted from the subject of Conrad, and that would give the fugitive more time to get deep into the cave and maybe out of the manhole. 'If Brodie had gotten the drop on you, he'd have killed you both.'

Kidd shrugged. 'Mebbe not — Chick an' me ain't exactly friends but he ain't mad at me bad enough to want to kill me. And with a bounty on Conrad, he'd want him taken in alive.'

'The hell he would! He claims

Conrad beat-up on him as well as Randy McLaren. Chick don't forget a thing like that.'

That gave Kidd his chance to keep them interested even longer while Conrad tried to find his way out of the cave. He shuffled his feet and hung his head, trying to look like a man who had been caught out lying.

'We-ell — things did get a mite lively between 'em. Not too sure how it happened, but next I know they's beatin' the hell outa each other and, cut a long story short, Conrad won.'

That caused a stir and some interest amongst the posse men. They had never heard of Chick Brodie losing a brawl before. Kidd made the most of it, getting into blow-by-blow descriptions until Tyrell stopped him irritably.

'Well, where's Chick and Conrad now? That's what I want to know. Right now, Kidd!'

'We lost Brodie,' Kidd muttered and gave a more-or-less honest account of how he had been trying to extract a broken tooth from Conrad's jaw hinge and Brodie had apparently come round while he was doing it and vamoosed.

'Neither of us noticed him sneakin' off, then next thing the damn mountain's afire and we had to vamoose, pronto. Like I said, lucky I stumbled on this cave.'

'I wonder just how *lucky* that was?' the sheriff allowed. 'Lucky for us we came to check out the fire. If it hadn't burned away some trees we mightn't've seen the cave at all. Tad, Green, go take a look in there. A good look.'

The two posse men hesitated, looking first at each other and then at Tyrell. 'S'pose he's in there, waitin'?' the man named Tad asked.

'That's what we want to find out, damnit!'

'Then you go find out,' Green, a Slash K man, said flatly. 'I ain't goin' in there.'

Kidd started to chuckle to himself as they went on arguing. *Go for your life, Conrad! You can walk halfway to San*

Antone while these idiots fuss amongst themselves.

Then suddenly all talk ceased as a voice drifted up the slope. At first it called a litte feebly for 'Help!' Then the next appeal was for the sheriff.

'Brad! Brad! I'm down here . . . on the slope. I need some help!'

'Godalmighty, that's Ali!' Tyrell exclaimed, and instantly wrenched his mount's head, almost unseating the startled Green. He jammed in his spurs and then stood in the stirrups. This enabled him to see over the tops of a line of burnt brush and saplings that hid the burned-out slope and the muddy waterhole below from his view.

His sister was standing twenty yards down, muddy, dripping, waving. She looked a mess — and exhausted.

'Come on! Lend a hand, you men!' Tyrell shouted over his shoulder, forgetting about Conrad and Kidd in his anxiety about the dishevelled Ali now trying to crawl up the slope.

Inside, Conrad cursed as he put his hand in a thick layer of bat manure on the wall, turning his head slightly so as to catch the draught and use it for direction. There was little light and he had barked his shins, banged his swollen hands and head, as well as both knees.

He had been working his way along the knife-blade, zig-zagging crevice in pitch darkness, afraid to strike a vesta — anyone could be following him, their sounds drowned out by his own small noises. Stones clattered, his gun rig scraped across rock, his spurs jingled but there wasn't room enough for him to stoop and remove them. He was breathing hard and his jaw ached like a mule had kicked him, but he kept on until he felt the direction of the draught change.

It angled upwards now, ruffled his thick hair hanging over his shirt collar, brushed his ears and battered face.

Tilting his head, he saw the outline of the exit hole above at the end of the shallow, upward-angling slope. Feeling a surge of confidence now, new energy flooding his throbbing body, he began the climb.

It was a lot less difficult than he expected: there were jutting rocks enough to make it almost a natural stairway in parts.

He paused near the top, straining to hear. Nothing seemed to be moving behind him down in the cave: there was a distant droning kind of noise, but he couldn't identify it. Above, he could see the sky, smell and taste the smoke from the fire, hear an occasional bird, likely returning to look for its nest or young.

He gripped a rock handhold and heaved with his legs. His head passed through easily but it was tight on his shoulders. He twisted his body, eased one arm and shoulder through first, flailed his legs until his boots found purchase and then thrust. His body eased forward and he thrust again

— and again until he squirmed almost all the way through on to a gravelly slope, his arrival lifting a cloud of burned leaves and grass stalks. He rested — and sneezed.

'I won't say 'Bless you!', 'cause I don't give a damn about you, Conrad,' a harsh voice said from nearby, and, as he twisted to see, he heard the click of a gun hammer being cocked. 'Was hopin' the fire woulda finished you and that skunk Kidd. Now I get to do it personal. I like that better!'

'You fire that gun, Brodie, you'll have Brad Tyrell breathing down your neck,' Conrad said, not moving now as he looked up at the battered man in the torn, singed and filthy clothes, standing a little unsteadily a few feet away. 'You don't look too good — get caught in your own fire?'

'Shut up!' Brodie wanted to slap him but was leery of getting too close. 'Lookin' for my hoss and found you instead comin' outa the ground. Never knew there was a cave hereabouts but now you're here it's a bonus. Where's the posse anyway? I couldn't see nothin' for smoke.'

'They're just down the slope; they oughta be here any time. They're plenty close enough to hear a gunshot.'

'Aah, they don't want me, you're the one they're after. They figure you beat an' stomped Randy McLaren.'

'Thanks to your lies. But go ahead and shoot. I can't stop you, but you'll have plenty of explaining to do to Tyrell and his posse.'

Brodie grinned with his smashed mouth, swollen eyes glittering. 'I'll rig it so you'll have a gun in your hand. It'll look good.'

'Not for me.'

Brodie laughed outright this time. 'Too bad you're a damn sodbuster, Conrad! I think I could get to like you some.'

'I'll be glad to live without your friendship, Chick.'

'Hell, you ain't gonna live at all!'

Brodie settled his boots firmly and

aimed his Colt at Conrad who tensed, wishing he wasn't lying on his right side: his body was pinning his upper arm and prevented him from getting at his six-gun.

Then Brad Tyrell's voice came echoing up the shaft behind him, booming and clear.

'Conrad? You up there blockin' the light? C'mon, man! Answer me! You've got no place to go now!'

'I'm here,' Conrad called quickly. 'Chick Brodie's holding a gun on me.'

A brief silence, then Tyrell again. 'Nice work, Chick! Hold him for a couple minutes — I got men ridin' up there right now.'

Brodie swore, curled a lip at Conrad. 'Sharp as a knife-point, ain't you, you bastard!'

'Chick!' the sheriff called again. 'I want him alive! I find him dead, you're in a heap of trouble.'

Brodie sighed, calling, 'He's OK, but I'd just as leave put a slug in him, Brad!'

'I told you what'll happen if you do . . . '

Then it was too late. The first of the posse came riding up the slope and over the small ridge towards the hole in the mountainside. There were four of them, all armed.

Conrad was relieved, but he wondered why the hell Kidd had told them about the escape route from the cave? He must have told them; Tyrell couldn't have known about it otherwise, and the posse wouldn't know where the hole came out into the open unless they had directions.

Surely that bounty money didn't mean that much to Kidd?

By then the posse men had closed in and he was ringed by weary, irritable riders with their fingers on the triggers of their weapons.

One said tersely, 'You can put your gun away, Chick, we'll take charge now.'

Brodie was reluctant but finally obeyed, looking more than a little worried.

★　　★　　★

Ali was waiting with Brad Tyrell and the remainder of his posse near the cave mouth when they brought in Conrad and Brodie.

Conrad was surprised to see her. At first he didn't recognize her, she was in such a mess, plastered with streaky mud and charcoal from the fire. Brodie dismounted slowly, frowning in her direction but she ignored him, came across to Conrad.

'I tried to reach Brad in time! Thank goodness you're OK.'

'I've been better,' he admitted, seeing her studying his injuries. He jerked a thumb towards Brodie. 'We had a few things to settle.'

Her eyes flicked to Brodie, then back to Conrad. 'I think Dog Beale has probably settled them for you.' She smiled through the grime at his puzzled expression, seeing Brodie out of the corner of her eye tense suddenly. 'Dog died, but on his deathbed he admitted telling a lie earlier.' She looked directly at Brodie now. 'He said it was Chick Brodie who beat-up Randy McLaren.'

'Dog said that?' Brodie growled. 'Man always was a damn liar! Or he was outa his head! Must've been. I never — '

'He confessed to Doc Moreno, Chick,' Brad Tyrell said quietly, as he covered Brodie with a cocked six-gun.

So that's why Kidd told Tyrell about the cave's exits. He knew it would be better for Tyrell to bring Conrad in now there was a real chance of him proving his innocence.

Brodie bristled. 'I don't care if he confessed to the Pope! He's a goddamn liar! An' — '

'Watch your mouth!' snapped Brad angrily. 'Doc Moreno's not one to lie and he's heard plenty of deathbed confessions so he wouldn't make a mistake. It works better with you bein' the villain, Chick. Just your style.'

'Aw, sure! I got a rep for fightin' so I'm the one to blame! Hell, I told you, and you must've seen the marks on my face, Conrad started in on me. Randy whateverhisname said he'd better go easy, that he was playin' too rough. Then Conrad told him to keep his nose outa his business and beat him to a pulp! Man's a maniac when he gets on the prod!'

Conrad started towards Brodie, but Tyrell moved between them, looking from one man to the other with hard eyes. 'I guess I gotta check this out a little more.'

'If it's any help,' Kidd said suddenly, 'Russ told me it was Brodie done the beatin'. Kinda thing Chick would do. Likes it when a man can't fight back.'

'Shut up, Kidd! I'll get to you sooner or later!'

'Make it later,' growled the sheriff. 'Green, McCann, hold Brodie while Kidd ties his hands behind him.' He swung towards Conrad. 'Then do the same to Conrad.'

'Brad!' gasped Ali, crossing to stand beside her brother. 'Russ is innocent! I told you!'

'Maybe, Ali. Yeah, I know Dog Beale was dyin', but maybe he didn't say that to help Conrad so much as to get back at Chick for leavin' him at the bottom of that cliff.'

'Yeah! That's more like what Dog'd do!' Brodie said eagerly. 'I really thought he was dead when I rode off, but Dog was a mean one. He coulda said I done that to Randy just to get back at me.'

Ali, tight-lipped, nodded, looked up at her brother. 'Doctor Moreno more or less said the same thing, Brad, I have to be honest about it.' Her gaze swung to Conrad. 'I'm sorry, Russ. I don't believe you beat-up Randy McClaren, but to be fair . . .'

Conrad scoffed barely audibly. 'Fair? Yeah — I guess. So what does this mean, Sheriff?'

'Means I'm holdin' you both in my cells till I look into things some more.'

Great! thought Conrad. *Just what I need — Chick Brodie for a cellmate!*

Then Ringo Magraw came riding out

of the burnt trees, both he and his horse showing obvious signs of having come in contact with the fire. It was still burning down in one of the draws but the wind had changed now and was blowing it on to broken, bare ground with only a few stunted bushes. It would be extinguished entirely within the hour.

'Where the hell'd you get to?' the sheriff demanded of Magraw. 'I told you to stick with us.'

Ringo shrugged. 'Wanted to catch up with Conrad myself. I found tracks and was followin' 'em in when suddenly the damn mountain's on fire an' I gotta ride like hell or get my hide singed.'

'When you're in my posse you do what I say!' snapped Tyrell, not letting it go. 'You go where I tell you, nowhere else.'

'Don't seem to matter now. *I* was the one found Conrad's tracks. Now I hear you say you ain't even sure he's the one put Randy in the infirmary!' His ash-smeared face hardened. 'What do I believe, Sheriff? Randy's my pard and this thing has to be settled.'

'It will be — my way. By the book. If you heard about Dog Beale's deathbed confession, then you know I have to investigate further. Personally, I lean towards Conrad bein' innocent, but I dunno much about him. He could be the meanest son of a — pardon Ali, forgot you was there. But you see what I mean, don't you, Ringo? I gotta be sure.'

Ringo lifted his slow hooded gaze to the lawman's face. 'I gotta be sure, too.'

'You stay out of it! It'll be done accordin' to law an' you poke your snoot in, I'll come down on you like a house cavin'-in!'

Ringo held the man's gaze a moment, said nothing, his expression unchanging as he turned to stare at Conrad and Brodie.

'One of you is guilty, and that means one of you is dead where you stand the moment I find out which it is! And the best way to do that, I reckon, is to ask Randy himself!'

Brad Tyrell started to speak, but Ringo wheeled his mount and rode off, down the slope towards the draw that would lead him back to the distant trail to town.

10

HOSTAGE

The old swing station at Columbia was due to close down soon and so the stage on the southern run was delayed. The crew at the station had little interest in a job they were soon to lose, with no prospects of further employment. At least according to the passengers, two men and three women, a mother and her two daughters, that's how it seemed.

It had been a hot, uncomfortable run out from Conifer Bend and it was getting hotter sitting in the dubious shade of the *ramada* on the crumbling adobe building. Inside was chaos as the lazy crew had been tearing out counters and stacking tables and generally making it hard for anyone to get comfortable. They had to eat the so-called meal out of grubby and banged-up tin platters on their laps. The youngest girl was crying because she had spilled so much chili sauce on her frock. The mother was scrubbing hard with a handkerchief dampened in the scummy horsetrough by the older girl. The two men sat on a log under a tree, sweating in their frockcoats, smoking.

They all looked up when the driver came around from the rear of the station building. Stooped and gnarled, bullwhip coiled and hanging from one sloping shoulder, he spat a stream of tobacco juice and announced, 'Underway in five minutes, folks. You be ready. I ain't waitin' for no one. Yonder's the privy. You want to use it, do it now. Long stretch from here to the next swing-station. They call the trail the Bladder-Buster . . . hahaha!'

The passengers needed no second telling and all were seated in the hot coach with its canvas blinds drawn against the hammering sun by the time the driver clambered up into the seat.

None of the station crew bothered seeing them off.

The stage rolled out with a half-dozen cracks of the bullwhip, salted with a few choice cusses the driver made no attempt to keep from the tender ears of the lady passengers.

There was no guard riding along, the company saving a few dollars. A guard wasn't needed anyway. There was nothing of value in the strong box, or the couple of well-worn mail sacks. The stageline was winding down fast and the driver was worried about what he would do. He knew nothing else and was too damned old to have much hope of finding a driving job with another line.

The old shotgun rattling around at his feet bounced and landed on his instep and he swore at it, almost reaching down to throw it away, but he settled back, letting the team take the steep slope at their own pace and began worrying about his future again — the one he didn't have.

That was possibly why he didn't see the horseman sitting his mount in the middle of the trail with a rifle held upright, butt on his thigh, finger through the trigger-guard.

When he did see the man, he hauled rein so fast and energetically that he pulled himself half upright out of his seat. The passengers below squealed and cussed, according to gender, at the brutal stop, the wheels skidding.

'What the hell you want?' the driver shouted at the rider, spitting to the side.

'Want your strongbox and your mail sacks — and whatever goodies your passengers are carryin'.'

'Hey, mister, this is a dry run for you. Nothin' in the strongbox 'cept bank papers and the mail sacks ain't hardly worth liftin'.'

'Throw down the box,' the rider said, and when he tilted his head some, out of the shadow of his wide-brimmed hat with the deep dent in the top, angling up from front to back, the driver saw he wore a bandanna masking the lower half of his face.

About then, two more riders came out of the rocks, one toting a shotgun. The passengers stepped down. One of the men began to bluster but shut up pronto when the first rider put a bullet into the ground a bare inch from his boots. He was the first to thrust up his hands shoulder high, saying, breathlessly to the others, 'Best do what they say, folks!'

For a moment, the robbers weren't watching the driver. He nudged the shotgun with his boot. If he could get it up, defend the coach, it would look good on his record and he was certain sure the company wouldn't fire him then.

It required instant decision and he reached down as if to get the strongbox but came up fumbling with the shotgun. Arthritic hands made him miss the hammer spur and by that time, the bandit who had straddled the trail saw him and the rifle swung down and fired. The single bullet picked up the driver and dropped him into the trailside brush.

'Damn old fool!' said the killer. He pointed the smoking rifle at the male passenger who had been blustering a few moments earlier. 'You — climb up and get that strongbox. Rest of you get out your valuables while we collect 'em. Come on, ladies! Be quick, or my men'll have to search you . . . ' He laughed briefly. 'See how fast you can move when you want to?'

The youngest girl began to cry and clung to her mother's skirts as the woman rummaged nervously in her large bag. The other girl, about thirteen, fair hair in pigtails, glared tight-lipped at the bandits. As she handed over her cheap bluestone bracelet to a masked man, she said, 'I hope you rot in hell! That old man never harmed anyone!'

Dark eyes glittered above the bandanna. 'Might've harmed you — you don't shut up talkin' about him.'

Her mother grabbed her daughter's

arm and shook her. 'Be quiet, Cassie! Please! Just be quiet!'

Cassie continued to glare as the men took the mail sacks, the money and wallets and junk jewellery, and mounted up. The leader shot the first horse in the team and nodded to his man who carried the double-barrelled shotgun.

This man shot out the spokes on a rear wheel and the coach jarred and sagged, a little luggage spilling from the roof rack. The women cowered and the shot-gunner laughed.

'Guess you got yourselves quite a walk, folks!'

★ ★ ★

Sheriff Brad Tyrell was halfway to the infirmary when a townsman came running across the street shouting his name, waving his hat.

Tyrell sighed. *What now?*

'What's all the fuss, Cam? I'm dead on my feet.'

'Not as dead as Calico Bill,' the

townsman gasped.

'Cal . . . ? That old stage driver's dead? What happened?'

'Stage was held up after leavin' the swing station at Columbia. He tried to save the strongbox but they shot him.'

'Judas Priest! As if I ain't got enough on my plate! Who brought the news?'

'Young gal, Cassie Weddemier . . . She cut a hoss outa the team, seems like, and rode in to tell us. Bareback, too. Her mother's still up there with the other passengers. Bandits wrecked the stage.'

Brad glanced towards the infirmary, saw a grim-faced Ringo Magraw coming out and walking his way. To the townsman, the sheriff said, 'Better organize some men and we'll go out there. Dammit all!' He raised his voice as Cam hurried away, some curious townsman calling to ask what was up. 'Ringo! Wait up!'

Ringo slowed, obviously reluctant, and waited as Brad came hurrying over. 'You see Randy?'

'Yeah. I saw him.' Flat and heavy, tight-lipped.

'Well! C'mon, for Chris'sakes, tell me what he said! I got a stage hold-up to attend to now.'

'He din' say nothin'.'

Tyrell tensed at the way the man said it and the look of thunder on his ugly face. 'He's . . . dead?'

Ringo's lips tightened. 'Might as well be. Still unconscious. Can't move, can't talk, can't feed hisself . . . '

'My God! Sorry to hear that. Well, I've got Brodie and Conrad locked up in separate cells. I'll get it settled when I get back. Don't s'pose you'd care to ride along?'

'I've done enough ridin' and traipsin' around this damn country. I'm gettin' myself some decent grub and a soft bed, then I'm quittin' this neck of the woods. You can keep it. Nothin' I can do for Randy now.'

He swung away and strode off down the street. Brad watched him go, feeling a mix of relief and uncertainty. He'd be glad to have Ringo out of the town but — it did seem a sudden turn-around after all his talk of vengeance.

'Sheriff!' someone called. 'We got six men waitin'.'

Tyrell shook himself, waved and strode quickly across the street to where Cam had gathered some angry-looking and armed townsmen near the livery. Link Weddemier was one.

Brad was so engrossed then with getting his rescue party organized that he didn't see Ringo Magraw pause in a doorway, lean his shoulders against the wall and begin to make a cigarette. He lit up and smoked slowly, watching Brad Tyrell lead his group towards the edge of town. At the same time he saw Ali Tyrell, now obviously bathed and changed, going into the infirmary, probably to enquire about Randy McLaren. *He'd better make his move — now!*

Ringo tossed his half-smoked cigarette away and tugged his hat down over his eyes as he made his way quickly towards the law office and jailhouse . . .

★ ★ ★

Brodie was restless, pacing his cell, swearing, kicking at the barred door. He turned and glared through the bars separating his cell from the one next door where Russ Conrad sprawled on his bunk, smoking. 'The hell you takin' it so easy for?'

Conrad didn't open his eyes. 'No point in knocking yourself around. You can't get out. Might's well make the most of the rest while you can.'

Brodie scowled. 'You're loco! You're in a helluva lot of trouble, drifter!'

'Nothing new. But if Randy's come around, you're the one in trouble.'

'Huh! Take the word of a half-witted man who's had his head kicked in against me and half-a-dozen of Keefer's riders? Don't get your hopes up, feller. The judge is a good friend of Keefer's! I ain't worried.'

175

Conrad said nothing more, took a drag on his cigarette and then the door at the end of the passage crashed back with a thud that made the barred cell doors rattle. Heavy, fast-striding boots approached and Conrad swung his legs over the bunk, tensed when he saw it was Ringo Magraw. He had his Colt in one hand, the ring of cell keys in the other. Brodie swore as the man approached, retreated to the far wall of his cell, apprehensive as Ringo paused at the door.

'You son of a bitch! Randy's come round and he just told me who it was beat the crap outa him!'

Brodie's face changed, suddenly accepting he was going to be the target of Ringo's anger.

'He's off his head with pain if he blamed me!'

Ringo, steaming, nostrils flared, shook his head slowly. 'No. He's fine now. Well, not fine; he's gonna be laid up for some time yet, but he'll make it, though he's gonna have some big problems.

Thanks to you, Brodie!'

He fumbled with the keyring and slid the key into the lock when there was a call from the front office.

'Ringo! Are you in here?'

Conrad recognized Ali Tyrell's voice and then she appeared at the end of the passage in her grey dress, her damp hair drawn back in a chignon, making her look older, he thought.

'Ali! Get back! There's trouble here! Best find your brother.'

She kept coming, watching Ringo. 'Brad's had to take some men out to Columbia. There's been a stage hold-up. Ringo, I just went to the infirmary to see how Randy is and I found him sitting up in bed, Mrs Moreno feeding him! Doctor Moreno said you'd been there and left after saying Randy wasn't even conscious. And I suspect you told Brad the same! I knew you'd come here! Please, don't do anything foolish!'

Ringo stared sullenly, hand still on the key, six-gun sagging down at his side now. 'Go away, ma'am. This ain't for you.'

'Who is it for?' she countered. 'Randy? Or you?'

'It's for both of us. I shoulda got here earlier and Randy wouldn't've been workin' for him.' He gestured into Conrad's cell but the girl didn't look at him. 'And he wouldn't've been beat-up! Now it's time to settle things!'

He turned the key and the lock's pins slipped back with a click. But, as he made to wrench the cell door open, Brodie came hurtling off the wall, slammed a boot against the bars and smashed the door full force into Ringo. Ali screamed as Magraw crashed into the opposite passage wall, his head making a dull sound as his hat fell off.

His knees sagged and Brodie moved like a striking snake, snatched the Colt from the man's hand and shot Ringo twice in the upper body. Ali ran at him and he thrust her away roughly, sending her sprawling.

As Magraw tumbled, Brodie whirled

and fired into Conrad's cell and Ali screamed again as Conrad was hurled back, spinning, crashing half across his bunk. He slid back, blood running down one side of his face, eyes shut. Ali stared in horror as he fell limply and didn't move.

'You . . . you murderer!' she cried, very pale as she stared at Brodie, not knowing what else to say. 'You're in more trouble than you've ever been in! Brad will issue orders for you to be shot on sight now!'

Brodie bared his teeth, took a step forward and grabbed her wrist, hauling her to her feet. Her efforts to pull away were futile against his strength. 'Brad might think twice about that if I have you along for company, sweetheart!'

Ali didn't waste breath on words. She swung at him with her free hand but her small fist only made Brodie laugh. He shook her, pulled her in close, twisting her arm and making her cry out. 'You'll be more friendly after a while. C'mon, let's get outta here before some townsman finds enough guts to come see what the shootin' was all about!'

He dragged her towards the front office and inside dropped the bar over the street door. Through the dusty window panes he could see folk gathering outside, tentatively approaching. He flung Ali roughly into the chair.

'Don't move, or I'll shoot you right here, you bitch!' he slurred, and she sat there, shaking and afraid, rubbing her strained wrist as he gathered guns and ammunition.

When someone knocked on the door and shouted, 'Everythin' all right in there?' Brodie put a shot high up, and through the window saw the crowd hurriedly disperse.

A minute later he was dragging the girl back down the passage to the rear entrance. Both of them stepped around Ringo's body and glanced briefly into Conrad's cell.

The man hadn't moved, a pool of blood now formed under his head;

more streaked his ashen face.

Ali gave a small sob as she was dragged to the rear door and hurled out into the yard. As she stumbled, Brodie, carrying rifle and cartridge belts in one hand, grabbed her with the other and propelled her towards the stables where Brad Tyrell kept his best horses.

11

NIGHT VISITORS

The rider called Green picked up his hat, the one with the deep dent in it at the front, angling upwards and becoming more shallow towards the back of the crown. He turned it in his hand and set it on the back of his head.

Fergus Keefer closed the safe door in his ranch office, stood up and tossed a chinking drawstring poke on to the desktop, gesturing to it casually. 'It's all in there. Pay off that fool Larrabee and see he clears the county. He talks too much when he's boozing. You're sure Hazard can keep his mouth shut?'

Green smiled crookedly as he jingled the rawhide bag of coins in his hand. 'This'll guarantee it.'

Keefer didn't smile. 'If it doesn't, change that gold for lead.' Green's smile faded, but he nodded jerkily. The rancher picked up the bundle of papers that Green had placed on his desk earlier, the ones from the Columbia stage strongbox. He took them to the fireplace where a small fire was already burning, and dropped them in one by one. He sighed. 'Now I feel better. There's no record at all that Conrad or anyone else ever filed on that land at Two-way Creek. You did well, Aaron.'

Green had already received his golden appreciation for leading the stage hold-up. 'Too bad about old Calico. Used to like his stories about the Pony Express days.'

Keefer grunted. 'Don't let me keep you from your supper. Burn the strongbox, and throw away the junk jewellery. I don't want any trace of that hold-up around here.'

Aaron Green shrugged and went out with the bag of money. 'I'll see to it, boss.'

He had barely closed the door when there was a tap on the glass doors behind the curtains leading to one of the big ranch-house balconies looking clear across the basin to the distant hills: a picturesque scene across the wide creek fringing their base. Keefer took his polished old Walker Colt from the desk drawer, walked across softly and yanked the curtains back, gun cocked and ready.

He arched his eyebrows and unlocked the door as he recognized Chick Brodie. 'They told me you were in jail,' he said, as Brodie stepped inside, looking hot and begrimed from hard riding.

'There's a lot more you need to know,' he said, closing the curtains behind him. 'A *lot* more.'

Keefer allowed him two drinks while he told what had happened, from the fight and the fire in the ranges to his arrest and Ringo's attempt to kill him.

'Where's the girl now?' Keefer asked, his tone and face giving nothing away.

Brodie hesitated, twirled his empty shot-glass between gnarled fingers and said quietly, 'A place I know.'

Keefer's eyes narrowed as Brodie looked up challengingly. 'Playing it close to your chest, huh?'

Brodie shrugged. 'Well, Ringo and Conrad are dead. I need some sort of ace in the hole.'

'Mmmm — well, I guess you had to kill those two, but it makes it hard for me to get the judge to do anything for you . . . But the girl's the only witness now, isn't she?'

Their gazes were steady on each other's face and after a while Brodie nodded. Keefer said no more, just poured another drink for them both.

'Randy McLaren,' Keefer said suddenly, and Brodie snapped up his head. 'Too bad he didn't die. Then Tyrell would still believe Conrad was the one beat-up on him.' He paused, let that sink in, saw Brodie's face slowly lighten with understanding. 'Ringo came to the jailhouse raging after he'd seen Randy who must've been in his last few hours, and told him Conrad was the one beat him up . . . Ringo shot and killed

Conrad and somehow you got his gun when he tried to shoot you and it went off, nailed Ringo, and you were able to reach the keys and . . . ' Keefer spread his hands.

'That might take some arrangin'.'

'Not if there're no witnesses and Randy himself has succumbed to his injuries. I mean, it's understandable you'd run after all that shooting in the jail. You couldn't be sure Ringo was dead and you wouldn't want him coming at you again. It could be worked, Chick.'

Brodie didn't really like it, but saw the possibilities. With a good deal of thought he just might get away with it.

'Aaron Green's a good man if you need a hand,' Keefer said persuasively. 'Here, let me refill your glass.'

'How do we explain the girl goin' missin'?'

Keefer allowed his impatience to show then, slammed down the bottle of rye on the table top. 'Godamnit! *Think* man! I'm not going to do it all for you!

But you get it done somehow! Then come back and see me . . . not before!'

* * *

Conrad's head ached and ached without let-up, despite the pain killer Doc Moreno had given him.

With his head bandaged, he lay there in the infirmary at the other end of the room from Randy McLaren and tried to sleep. But the pain wouldn't let sleep come. The doctor told him he was a mighty lucky man: the bullet had burned across his scalp, just deep enough to knock him out and produce a fair amount of blood. The thickness of a cigarette paper deeper and it would have blown a great slab of bone from his skull and let his brains ooze out.

'As it is,' Moreno said, as he carefully dressed the wound while the groggy Conrad gripped the edge of the bed to keep from falling, 'you'll have to put up with a headache for a few days, maybe some vision disturbances, certainly some nausea, but then you should recover completely.'

Well, the sawbones was sure right about the damn headache! It was like the big brother of all hangovers, showing no signs of diminishing. His clothes and gun rig and warbag had been brought in and now rested on the chair beside the bed. For a wild moment he thought of getting dressed and taking a walk in the night air. See if that would help. Which only showed you how out-of-kilter his thinking was! Randy McLaren was snoring gently, moaning now and again, still in much pain from his injuries, especially his broken hands. They were the only two patients right now. There had been a townsman who had just recovered from a bout of lung fevers but he had gone home just before dark, half-dragged out by a bitter-faced woman who never stopped telling him about all the odd jobs that had accumulated at home while he was in the infirmary, 'being waited on hand and foot!'

Conrad managed a thin smile: bet the poor devil wishes he was still in here. Idly, he glanced down at the bed the man had occupied in the middle of the row.

Then he stiffened.

There was a window above the row of beds, almost directly behind the one he had been looking at. *And there was a shadow on the smeared glass which began to slide up even as Conrad watched.* A man's shadow — a man holding a six-gun.

Conrad didn't think, just reacted instinctively. Forgetting about his throbbing head, he reached out to the chair, groped under the pile of clothes for his Colt. The clothes fell, made a soft *plop!* just as the window opened silently.

The man there froze with one leg halfway through. Then he must have seen Conrad swinging his legs over the side of the bed and the gun turned towards him and triggered. Conrad dropped to the floor, rolled, feeling a wave of dizziness break over him even as he brought up his own Colt.

The intruder triggered again and the lead thudded into the mattress just above Conrad. He fired three fast shots. Glass shattered, a man grunted and then a body tumbled into the room. Someone cursed — someone outside!

There were two of them!

Conrad fired again and splinters flew from the window frame and more shards of glass tinkled. Someone swore. There was the sound of something falling and then the muffled thudding of retreating boots beyond the shattered window.

The one on the floor wasn't finished yet. Half-sitting he triggered again, but the shot was wild and went into the wall high above Conrad's bed. Conrad fired under the empty beds in front of him to where the killer lay stretched out, bleeding, two beds distant. The body jerked and there was a groaning grunt, the clatter of a six-gun falling . . .

'The dang hell's goin' on?' That was Randy McLaren, struggling to sit up.

'Hell almighty!' he added as Conrad groped his way to his bed. The door burst open and a sleep-dishevelled Dr Moreno charged in, a pepperbox pistol in his hand. But the weapon wasn't even cocked and the medic looked bewildered.

'Better get the sheriff, Doc,' Conrad panted, sagging now, rubbing at his head with one hand.

'He's been investigating the stage hold-up at Columbia. I sent him word about his sister disappearing but he can't get back before morning.'

'Well, that one won't be going anywhere.' Conrad indicated the dead intruder and the doctor, lighting a lamp now, stooped and let the light wash over the bloody corpse.

'I believe that's — that's Aaron Green. The Slash K mustanger.'

'Hell, I don't know him,' Randy said, shaken by the shooting, voice slurred. 'What the hell was he tryin' to do?'

Conrad, thinking despite his head-ache, said slowly, 'Well, I guess he was after one of us . . . maybe both.'

Townsmen arrived and eventually the dead man was taken away. Then the doctor checked Conrad's wound and replaced the bandages with a square of lint held on by adhesive tape. It pulled and tugged at Conrad's hair but it was preferable to the tight swathe of cloth.

'You'd both better get some rest,' Moreno said. He looked down at Conrad. 'I'll give you a sleeping draught, or another pain killer if you want.'

Conrad hesitated, then shook his head slightly. 'No thanks, Doc. I hate this kind of woozy feeling all the time, like I'm not in control.'

Moreno frowned slightly. 'You'll have to put up with the headache then. It could get a lot worse.'

'I dunno how! No, Doc, I'll be all right. I'll rest up a spell.'

Moreno didn't look really convinced but went to tend to Randy McLaren who was very white now and complained of nausea. He was far from making total recovery yet awhile.

'That's the concussion,' the medic told him. 'You'll be some time before you get over that . . . I'll definitely give you a sleeping draught. It'll see you through the pain.'

After he had finished, he asked Conrad again if he had changed his mind. When the man said he hadn't, he went out shaking his head.

'You really think they were tryin' to kill us?' McLaren asked, his words already slurring because of the sleeping draught. When Conrad grunted, he asked, 'Why?'

'You told Ringo that it was Brodie who beat you. Doc Moreno took Ringo's word that you were still unconscious and hadn't told him anything. Brodie thought I was already dead, and he'd taken the girl with him so that only left you. They were likely gonna hold a pillow over your face, try and make it look like you'd passed away in your sleep.'

'Aw, geez . . . I reckon I'll be awake

all night now, a'worryin'! I . . . ' In moments Randy was snoring.

That second man had almost certainly been Brodie, Conrad thought, the one outside, sending in Green first, playing it safe as usual. Which meant he must have stashed Ali Tyrell somewhere — or had already killed her.

He felt the goosebumps prickle his skin at the thought. *She'd tried to save his life, divert Brodie's gun in that cellblock passage.* It didn't set easy, Brodie taking her hostage, or somewhere out of town to kill her because she was the only surviving witness who knew he was the one who beat Randy. That would only leave Randy himself, but they'd likely have shot Doc Moreno just to be on the safe side. They might even make another try!

Hell, he couldn't just lie here! There was a slim chance that Ali might still be alive! He had to do something.

He sure didn't feel a hundred per cent, but he had to get out of here before Brad Tyrell returned. The damn sheriff was so cautious he could even throw Conrad back in the cells *for his own safety*, or some other such nonsense.

Conrad didn't aim to sit still for that. He had to try even if it killed him.

★　★　★

She was terrified. It was dark and dank and smelled of animals. She was bound hand and foot as well as gagged.

Nothing like this had ever happened to her before. She wasn't even sure what she was terrified of most. Dying? Rape? A physical beating? For Brodie sure hadn't been gentle with her so far. He had yanked her off her horse, flung her across his shoulder and brought her in here holding a handful of burning brush to find his way.

She thought it was one of the old abandoned mines in the foothills of the Catamounts, but it might have been a cave. He had dropped her on to the moist earthen floor, fumbled roughly at her clothing while he tied her up and gagged her, then pushed her back against another wall where protruding rocks cut into her back.

Without a word, he kicked out the glowing remains of the torch he had used and then he was gone.

It took a long while for her heart to settle down and just as it did and she tried to take some note of her surroundings, she froze, feeling the terror choking her.

Something had moved not more than a few feet from her in a pitch-black corner. Something that *slithered*!

* * *

Brad Tyrell looked like hell, haggard and red-eyed, dusty and begrimed from hard trails up in the hills and long hours of riding to get back to Conifer Bend after receiving word about Ali and Brodie's breakout.

He went straight to Moreno's and

together they found that Conrad was missing. It was barely daylight.

The sheriff made for the snoring Randy's bed and started to shake him by the arm without any effect.

'Leave him be, Brad! I gave him a sleeping draught,' the weary doctor said. 'He's in no state for questioning.'

'Where the hell has Conrad gone?'

Moreno started to shake his head. 'Oh! Maybe he's gone looking for your sister — he seemed upset to know she's been missing since the shooting at the jail.'

Brad scrubbed a hand down his haggard face, unsuccessfully tried to stifle a yawn. 'I'll fall outa the damn saddle I try to go after Conrad right now. You got somethin' to wake me up, Doc?'

'You'll be better resting, Brad — I mean it. I can give you a stimulant but once it wears off — and it wouldn't take more than a couple of hours — you'll drop like a falling tree, no matter where you are, or what you're doing. That could be dangerous for what you have in mind.'

Brad swore. 'All right. Look, I'll sleep right here, OK? You wake me in two hours at the most. I mean it, wake me up! Don't let me sleep past two hours. Then I'll get cleaned up and fed and start after Conrad.'

'You won't know where he's gone!'

'I reckon he'll go after Brodie — and I know where *he'll* go. Doc, I — I'm going to have to lie down, sorry about your clean sheets . . . '

He almost collapsed on the nearest bed, his dirt-caked boots swinging up and soiling the spotless top sheet.

Moreno sighed, loosened the man's gunbelt and shirt collar, then went out. His wife would chew him out when she saw that sheet. Then he brightened.

In two hours, he'd send *her* in to wake the sheriff.

Let Brad Tyrell explain about the sheets to his wife.

12

TRACKERS

It was still dark when Conrad left the town's limits. He had rested reasonably well but the headache was still there, though slightly diminished.

He felt shaky, but ignored this: he knew all about reaction after battle and being wounded. It would pass and to dwell on it would only stop him from thinking clearly about what he was going to do.

That was it: *what was he going to do?* He knew what he *had* to do — find and rescue Ali Tyrell. Killing Brodie was high on the list but getting the girl away safely had to have top priority. Brodie would more than likely contact Keefer again, but he didn't think they would hold Ali on Slash K land. Keefer was more cautious — and smarter — than that.

Also, Keefer would sacrifice Brodie and Ali if he had to, he had no doubt about that. Conrad didn't know the damn country well enough, that was his big problem. Brodie had been riding this basin and its surrounding ranges for years and knew a hundred places where he could hold a prisoner safely. Russ Conrad knew very little of it. There were no tracks, of course: any that might have been left by Brodie in his flight from the jailhouse had long ago been trampled and marred by the posse and other travellers using the trail in and out of town.

Maybe his leaving the infirmary was premature. *No!* He had to go when he did. *Had* to. He needed light to see by for one thing, but the restlessness in him wouldn't have allowed him to stay any longer. He and Randy McLaren had been targets and to him that meant that Brodie, maybe on Keefer's orders, though possibly acting alone, aimed to kill everyone who could point the finger at him for beating-up Randy.

He was in the hills already when it started getting light, the sky paling first, then cloud-reflected early sun rays casting fuzzy shadows and finally the blinding spears of fast-approaching full daylight.

That was when he realized he was being followed.

It hit him suddenly and hard, harder than it should have, and he knew he was still not operating at a hundred per cent efficiency. Quickly, he pulled the buckskin, now rested and fed, into the brush, slid the Winchester from the saddle scabbard and watched the bend of the trail where it rose out of a dry wash. It was there he had heard the clink of horseshoes against the loose shale and, as he strained to see, he thought there was a faint haze of dust lifting lazily from the wash: hard to tell in this half-light.

He worked the rifle lever slowly, silently, feeling his heart against his ribs, blinking in an effort to get sharper vision. But it was still slightly blurred and he figured he would have to settle for that. He lifted the rifle, sighted down the barrel just above that rise where the trail lifted. He could hear the horse now — waited — waited for the rider's head to appear, finger curled lightly on the trigger.

Then just as he saw the horse — riderless! — a voice behind him said casually, 'Figured you had better hearin'.'

Conrad almost fell from the saddle, he whirled so fast, and set the dizziness swirling through his head. The rifle came around and down and he only just managed to stop from firing in time.

'Goddamnit, Kidd! You near gave me a heart attack! And I almost shot you!'

'You'd be dead if my name was Brodie,' Kidd said with a crooked smile. 'You don't look too spry.'

'No. What're you doing here?'

'Word travels fast through the basin. Heard about Ringo and the jailbreak, then the fracas at the infirmary and I said to myself, 'Kidd, that Conrad just can't stay away from trouble. You better go lend a hand'.'

'Right kind of you,' Conrad said, his heart only just now beginning to settle. He uncocked the rifle and slid it back into the scabbard as Kidd stepped out and caught the reins of his sorrel as it came over to him. 'Got that hoss well trained.'

'Plenty of time to do it.' Kidd absently stroked the animal's muzzle. 'You're lookin' for Brodie, right?'

Conrad nodded. 'Might be being a little foolish but I've got to do something to help the girl.'

'Sure. Knew you'd be thinkin' that way. Brodie went out to Slash K. He didn't have the gal with him.'

Conrad looked at him sharply. 'You saw him?'

Kidd nodded. 'Was doin' a little scoutin' — lookin' for mavericks.' He winked. 'Seen Brodie come in from the direction of the Catamounts. His hoss looked like it'd put a lot of miles behind it.'

Conrad glanced towards the Cata-mount Hills. 'Was hoping he wouldn't go in there. Kinda wild for the way I'm feeling.'

'Well, if the gal's still alive, I reckon he's got her hidden away someplace in there.'

'She better be alive!'

'Take it easy. With a snake like Brodie, you can never tell how he's thinkin'. Cunnin' as a packrat, mean as a rattler — he does what he figures is best for the moment, worry about the right or wrong later.'

'Guess you're right.'

Kidd squinted at Conrad, noting the grey touch to his face, the drawn, deep-etched lines of pain and the reddened eyes. 'You did good to nail Aaron Green, but you ask me you oughta stayed in the infirmary.'

'Don't you start!'

Kidd grinned. 'Ol' Doc been ridin' you some, has he? Yeah, well, I savvy why you're here and the two of us ought to be able to do somethin'. Savin' the gal is the main thing with you, uh? You can kill Brodie later.'

'That's something you can bet on.'

'Thought so — Sir Gallyhad, or whatever that feller's name was, went around rescuin' damsels in distress.' He lifted his hands, palms out, as Conrad started to say something. 'It's OK, it's OK — I know that's how you was brought up. Only thing amazes me is you've lived so long. But that in itself must say somethin' about you, huh?' He laughed shortly. 'Quit lookin' so worried and let's figure out our next move, OK?'

Conrad sighed and nodded, rubbing his forehead. 'Feels like I got a drum in there somewhere. We better get going, do something. Moreno sent word up to Columbia station for Brad Tyrell and he'll be coming back hell-for-leather. He sees me he's just as likely to throw me back in jail till he can get round to questioning me.'

'Columbia? That stage hold-up? I heard whoever did it got nothin'.

Bunch of amateurs. Took a strong-box with nothin' but bank papers and such in it, the mail bags with no more'n a dozen letters, and a lotta junk jewellery and maybe thirty dollars from the passengers.' He shook his head. 'Killed poor old Calico Bill, the driver, for trash like that.'

Something stirred in Conrad's throbbing brain, but he couldn't grasp it and then Kidd mounted and led the way through the brush along a hidden trail Conrad didn't even know was there, towards the Catamounts, the slopes now aglow with the gold of early morning.

'You know where we're going?' Conrad asked.

'No — but there's a lot of places where a man could hold a prisoner. We'll check 'em out. You up to it?'

'Whatever it takes.'

A little later, they were riding down a twisting trail that dropped towards the shadowed cleft between the hills. Conrad's head was swinging side to side and studying the ground they passed over and ahead.

'You lookin' for tracks?' asked Kidd.

'I don't see you looking.'

'Well, if you think you'll find Brodie's sign, you're wastin' your time.'

'Then what're we doing here?' Conrad's voice was edgy.

'Tryin' to find the gal — Brodie's still back at Slash K.'

Conrad reined in sharply. 'He's what?'

Kidd hipped in the saddle, kept his horse going at walking pace. 'Sure. He hadn't left there when I come lookin' for you. Mebbe I'm guessin', but I reckon he's still there.'

'Damn you, Kidd! We can hole-up somewhere and wait for him to come by — follow him to where he's got Ali.'

'You think so? Conrad, that head-shot's addled your brain. Brodie don't make mistakes like that. I admit, the idea of jumpin' him is fine, but *doin*' it is somethin' else. 'Sides, he'll likely bring a couple Slash K hard-cases with him this time.'

'I'm not worried about the odds.'

'Me neither, but we could find the girl first, then bushwhack him and whoever's with him. We might kill him if we ambush him first, then we'd never know where he's hid her.'

'We don't know that now.'

'So we search while we've got a chance.' Kidd frowned slightly. 'This is gettin' to you, ain't it? You kinda sweet on Ali Tyrell?'

Conrad's head came up and he blinked. The denial caught in his throat. He hadn't even considered such a thing, but he suddenly realized he did care for Ali. She was only regular in the looks department, but it was her personality that attracted him. Her helpfulness, no condescending manner when she realized he could barely write his name; the way she had ridden out to search for her brother and tell him that Randy McLaren said it wasn't Conrad who had beaten him.

'I — don't want anything to happen to her. Specially not at the hands of someone like Brodie,' he said finally.

Kidd continued to stare and then nodded briefly. 'We better get along before Brodie shows up. He sees us, he won't go nowhere near where he's holdin' her.'

Conrad hesitated briefly, then followed Kidd down the steepening trail. The rustler was probably right and he needed the man to guide him through this wilderness.

He only hoped they would find Ali Tyrell safe and sound before something happened to her either at Brodie's hands or from some danger where she was imprisoned.

They didn't call these hills the Catamounts for nothing. And Kidd told him there were many snakes.

*   *   *

Keefer's face was set into hard lines and his eyes had the look of bullets in a cocked pistol. He continued to stare at Chick Brodie but the big man didn't seem unduly worried.

'I told you not to come here until you'd taken care of things,' the rancher said, mildly enough, but there was an underlying touch of steel in his words. 'You not only hadn't killed Conrad as you claimed, *he* killed our best man!'

'Green wasn't that good.'

'He was *good*!' Keefer emphasized his claim by slamming his open hand down on the edge of his desk, making some papers lift and slide. He ignored them, piercing gaze finally making Brodie show a little apprehension.

'OK, OK! He had a little luck is how I see it, but you want to think he was *good*' — he shrugged — 'don't really matter now, does it?'

'No.' Keefer sat down at his desk slowly, still glaring. 'You should've finished Conrad. If the man was still in the infirmary, he couldn't be entirely fit. Instead, you chose to run back here with your tail between your legs.'

That got to Brodie and he leaned his big, grizzled hands on his side of the desk, bending forward.

'You weren't there!' He said it flatly, challengingly. 'You're never *there*. You're always back here, or in some fancy hotel room with a high-class whore while me and the boys are *there*, wherever you send us!'

'That's what I pay you for,' Keefer told him in a low, dangerous voice. 'Now be careful, Chick. Be damn careful!'

'We do our best and most times — *most times* — we pull it off. Sometimes, we just can't do it. You weigh up one agin the other and you'll find you get just what you want about nine times outa ten.' He waited, but Keefer said nothing, merely continued to rake him with that bleak gaze. Then, surprisingly, Brodie smiled crookedly. 'And sometimes it ain't even our fault, it's your own.'

'What're you talking about?' Keefer demanded.

'The land at Two-way Creek. You had plenty time to file on that. Too blamed arrogant, so you just went ahead and used it illegally. No one cared much because no one else wanted it — till Conrad showed up. He went and filed on it right under your nose! That's what's really gallin' you, ain't it? Some drifter rides in and spits in your eye. That's it, ain't it? Someone outsmarted you and you can't abide it!'

Keefer leaned back in his chair, looking up at his ramrod, resting his elbows on the walnut arms of the chair, peaking his fingers together.

'Maybe you've got more brains than I gave you credit for, Chick. Yes, I'm riled at Conrad, plenty riled. But I'm a damn sight more riled at you and the others who fouled up a simple plan to get rid of him and give me that land! Men are dead now, there's a woman who's well liked in the community being held hostage somewhere in the wilds, and *Conrad is still alive!* Now, why wouldn't I be riled?'

Brodie shrugged his wide shoulders, straightening now. 'Sure, you got every right to be, but we done our best. And all of us — includin' you — underestimated this damn drifter! That's where the problem lies, boss, we took him for a pushover like Charley Reece and all the others, but this one's not only stubborn, he can fight back, too, and he ain't afraid to take on all of Slash K.'

Keefer appeared to think about that for a while and then he said, lowering his arms now and tapping his fingers lightly on the desk edge, 'And we're not going to beat the son of a bitch if we fight amongst ourselves — is that what you're trying to tell me, Chick?'

'That and a few other home truths. I'm on the run now. I got more to lose than I used to. We not only got to close that gal's mouth, we got to take care of her brother, and in case you've forgotten, slow though he might be, Brad Tyrell is the law around these parts.'

Keefer happened to be staring out of the window at this moment and Brodie saw him stiffen. Then the rancher turned his head slowly and smiled tightly at Chick.

'Speak of the devil . . . '

Brodie stepped to the window in two long strides, kept to one side and looked through the curtains flapping slightly in the morning breeze. 'Damn!'

Brad Tyrell was riding slowly into the ranch yard. The slanted sun's rays flashed brightly from the lawman's star on his shirt front.

'I gotta get outa here!'

Brodie started for the side door but Keefer snapped, 'Stay put — he'll see you. Once you're running he'll know something's wrong.'

'Christ! He knows that now, or he wouldn't be here!'

'Brazen it out, Chick! No one saw you take the girl hostage. Play the injured party! Hell, you were already in jail when this Ringo came in trying to kill you. Sure, you fought back, who wouldn't? One of the bullets must've ricochetted and got Conrad — lucky it didn't kill him. Ali? What about her?

You know nothing. She ran out of the jail after she said you should wait for Brad's return — you just cleared town fast as you could. You don't know what happened to her after that. It'll work, Chick!'

A glimmer of hope lifted in Brodie's chest but could he pull it off? Was Brad that gullible? Then —

'Judas priest! It's too damn late now, anyway! He's dismountin' at the porch!'

'Here.' Keefer handed the surprised ramrod a glass of whiskey, held one himself. 'Sit down, we're just having a quiet drink, discussing the situation, when Tyrell comes in. No one's nervous. Everything's fine. Just tell it the way I said and you'll be fine, too, Chick. Guarantee it.'

'Then what? If it does work, I mean.'

Keefer sighed. 'You go to the girl and have her make out a land file form in my name: I have some blanks, Todd — er — acquired some when I sent him in to the Land Agency to tear the page that listed Conrad's file number out of the register.'

Brodie stared, half-listening to Brad Tyrell stomping up on to the porch. 'I ain't even gonna ask what happens to the girl after that.'

Keefer smiled thinly. 'No need, is there?' The door opened and the hard-travelled sheriff came in. Keefer's smile broadened. 'Ah, Brad, thought that was you riding across the yard. Come in, come in, and have some of my bonded whiskey — you look like you can do with a double!'

The sheriff dropped into a chair, looking hard at Brodie. 'I can do with more than that. I'm here to find out what's happened to my sister and whatever story you've got worked out, Brodie, it better be damn good!'

Brodie blinked, making himself look bewildered. 'Your sister . . . ? I dunno nothin' about her.'

Brad sipped the whiskey slowly. 'So that's the way you want to play it.'

Brodie frowned, shaking his head

slowly. 'I don't wanta play it any way at all. I dunno where your sister is.'

Brad shifted his gaze to Keefer who was looking neutral right now. He held out his glass. 'You better hit me with another, Fergus, I can see this is gonna take some time — and I'm here for the long haul!'

13

DEADFALL

It was still there, far back in the shadows where the earth was damp and cool and there was also a fallen shoring post that had rotted, affording good protection should it be needed. Roof bracing dangled precariously.

She knew it was a snake — and a big one. These old abandoned mine shafts were full of them, made ideal habitats with their cool dankness and isolation. She could hear its scales sliding as it changed position slightly. Once, when she dozed a little, she thought it coughed but she had never heard of a snake doing that so she put it down to something she had been dreaming and couldn't quite recover.

The ropes were cutting into her wrists and ankles and the gag made her nauseous. She struggled but was afraid to move too much in case it enticed the snake in closer. Maybe it was a mother protecting her young. She shuddered and made a small moaning sound behind the gag: young, curious, adventuring snakes, slithering around, sensing the folds of her now grubby skirt in whatever way they sensed such things, coming closer to investigate the cloth that draped around the warm flesh of her legs . . . She whipped her legs up close to her chest as tightly as she was able.

Then, despite her resolve, unable to help herself now, she started to scream behind the gag, the sound muffled. Though there was a small echo from the old shaft that took a crooked bend some yards in from the entrance. Little sunlight reached into the second section where she was.

Oh, God! How long had she been here? Sleep — catnaps, really — had been intermittent. There was so little natural light that she couldn't be sure if it was early morning or the remains of moonlight. The moon had been shining when Brodie had dumped her in here. He had given her a mouthful of water first before gagging her, said nothing, just disappeared.

Leaving her alone with her thoughts. No! *Not alone* — that *was still there! That* thing.

Just waiting to strike. This time the scream turned to a sob and she fell on to her side. Panic struck like a lightning bolt and she moaned and screamed and thrashed frantically. Futilely. *Making far too much noise!*

Breathless, exhausted, she lay there, fighting the urge to move. And above the roaring of her breathing through distended nostrils and the thundering of her heart, she heard the slithering sound coming closer . . . closer. She could smell the reptilian body now, heard a kind of rasping hiss and felt a cold weight moving over her ankle . . . climbing.

Perhaps mercifully, she fainted.

★ ★ ★

Kidd could see that riding in country as rough as this was taking its toll on Conrad. The man must be suffering: there was fresh blood showing through the lint patch on his wound, his hat tilted to one side so there would be less pressure on it. He squinted all the time and Kidd knew the headache must still be with him. But no complaints.

Whenever Kidd suggested they take it easy for a spell, rest up for a smoke, Conrad merely shook his head, heeled his weary buckskin forward. Sighing, Kidd followed.

'Thought you knew this country?' Conrad snapped, as they turned out of a small blind canyon, the irritability in itself a sign the search was getting to him.

'Pretty well.'

'Well, it ain't well enough! Mid-morning and no sign. No — damn — sign! Not even tracks. Nothing at all to go on!'

'Brodie knows this country near as well as me. Told you he won't leave tracks that're easy to find.'

Conrad scowled. 'Told me this, told me that! Christ, Kidd, we dunno what she's suffering!'

'Or that she's sufferin' at all,' Kidd reminded him gently, and saw that craggy jaw jut a little more and the reddened eyes narrow.

'No. I feel she's still alive,' Conrad told him, more quietly now. 'But we have to find her, pronto! Look around, can't you see anything that tells where he could hide her?'

'We've checked all the caves I know. The draws and overhangs. That abandoned shack at the end of the wash is all that's left of the old minin' camp used to be here. Nothin' else survived from that. Most of the prospectors lived in tents or out in the open. Runnin' outa places, Russ.'

'What about the mines themselves?'

Kidd shook his head. 'Most of 'em collapsed. There was a rock-fault of some kind where they found the gold and the blastin' by the miners jarred it loose and filled most of the shafts, left others too damn unsafe to work. After a couple died in rockfalls, they abandoned the whole field.'

Conrad's gaze sharpened. 'But there're still mine shafts open?'

'A few, but not even animals hole-up in them. Liable to collapse if someone sneezes.'

'Dammit, Kidd! You think a man like Brodie'd worry about that? Solve a lot of his problems if a mine collapsed and buried Ali under half the mountain!'

Kidd's face was tight now. 'Hold on! I dunno. They crumble and tumble of their own accord . . . I've rid by places where there's no sign there was ever a mine shaft there, yet a week before I'd seen it gapin' like a scatter-gun's barrel.'

'Let's take a look!'

Kidd nodded suddenly, face still grim, but the expression now telling Conrad the man knew it was something he should have checked, no matter how unsafe the old mines were said to be.

They were almost buried alive in the second tunnel entrance they explored. A big rattler, rearing up on a huge pile of coils, struck at Kidd with fangs dripping and spade-head slashing. Kidd jumped back, instinctively drew and fired his pistol all in one motion. He missed the snake but the gunshot bounced and echoed from the shaky walls and before they could turn and run for the entrance, tons of earth and rock came showering down around them.

Somehow they managed to roll outside as choking dust, flying rocks and spewing earth pursued them only a few feet behind. There was a slope that dropped away suddenly and they skidded over this and lay there as raw earth piled up around and over them, subsiding gradually.

Gagging, ears ringing, they crawled out from under the layer of soil and sat there, blinking, looking up at the scarred mountain face. Kidd helped Conrad up.

'You say 'I told you so' and I'll shoot you and bury you in that loose dirt!' Conrad threatened, dusting himself down. He was groggy and unsteady, but he was alive. In a more friendly tone he added, 'Close!'

'Hope Brodie never heard the shot.'

'Don't think so. We were some yards in and you'd hardly fired when the whole kit and caboodle came down. It would've masked it.'

Kidd, his face grimy with dirt, spat some muddy saliva and asked, 'You want to look in the others?' A look from Conrad and he nodded jerkily. 'Yeah, 'course you do! OK, but I've never knowed anyone with a death-wish before.'

The next tunnel only went into the hillside about ten feet and they were met with a wall of collapsed rock and piled dirt and shattered timbers. The one after that was no more than a shallow cave. Kidd said he knew of only one more shaft in this section and wasn't sure, but thought the other area that had been prospected was totally obliterated.

So they went to investigate the one remaining tunnel Kidd knew about.

It was much deeper than the others and, on the slope outside, Conrad spotted a place where a small dead bush had had some branches broken from it recently. Very recently.

'For a torch mebbe? To see inside?'

'We could look for horse sign, too — '

'And waste time while Ali might be in there?'

Kidd knew by now there was no arguing with this tough drifter and nodded briefly, climbing up the short slope. They saw right away that there was a dog-leg bend in the shaft about five yards in.

'We're gonna need a torch, too,' Kidd said and started back down towards a dead bush.

When he looked up, holding a handful and fumbling for a match, he saw that Conrad had already entered the shaft. He hurried up, lit the torch at the entrance and strode towards the elbow bend. 'Conrad? Wait for some light — '

Then his stomach knotted and his heart skipped a beat *as two thundering gunshots sounded from around the elbow in the shaft!* 'Aw, God almighty!' he groaned. 'Not again!'

He glanced at the entrance outlined behind him as if it was his last look at pure sunlight, then, torch burning, stepped around the bend.

Conrad was hurrying towards him, smoking pistol in one hand, Ali Tyrell, bound and gagged and mighty muddy, slung over a shoulder. Kidd dropped the torch where it burned and still dimly lit the shaft. Ears cocked for the first sounds of avalanche or collapsing ancient tunnel braces, he reached forward and took some of Ali's weight.

They were outside in seconds and still there was no sounds of a collapsing tunnel as they stopped where they had left the horses. Conrad went down on one knee and Kidd helped him lay the girl down as gently as they could. He snapped his head around to Conrad.

'Is she alive?'

Conrad, breathing heavily, rubbing at his throbbing temple, nodded. 'Just out cold, I think.'

'The hell were you shootin' at?'

'Not sure if it was a big packrat or a monitor lizard. Was doing something to her lower leg.'

'Coulda been another snake.'

'No — it was a different shape. Eyes seemed to glow, so likely was a lizard. She coulda mistook it for a snake, though, panicked and passed out . . . '

'You could've brought down the whole damn tunnel!'

Conrad suddenly bared his teeth in a taut grin. 'Twice lucky in the one day, huh?'

'Jeessuss!' Kidd breathed, and it was more a sigh of gratitude than a blasphemy.

★ ★ ★

Chick Brodie had three men riding with him. Todd, Tad Hazard and a man known simply as 'Wolf' — first name, last name, nickname, no one knew.

But he was as mean, as cunning and as lethal as his namesake. Especially when he was being paid well, as he was this time.

As soon as Brodie had told him there was to be a fifty dollar bonus per man, Wolf knew that whatever the chore, it was important to Keefer. He always made a note of these 'special' jobs: there could come a time when the knowledge might buy him out of trouble. Of course, such knowledge could also earn him a bullet, but Wolf was a man who was prepared to take risks if the reward seemed big enough.

And a man's own life was about as big as you could get.

Hazard was easy-going: slip an extra dollar into his pay packet and he was a happy man. An extra dollar meant extra time in Rio Sadie's Pleasure Pit. Todd — well, Todd was one of the silent ones.

Said little, absorbed much, and you never knew which way he was going to jump. But he was good with a gun and didn't mind beating-up man or woman.

It was a tough quartet that rode into the Catamounts through the hot white sunshine, hellbent on murder . . . men whose only loyalty was to themselves.

Chick Brodie had been going to come alone to the place he had stashed Ali Tyrell, but Keefer said he wanted this job done and done well. 'Clean, Chick. No dirt or muck left around that could be raked over and land on my door stoop. Take two or three men and clean it up, leave no trace at all. You savvy what I'm saying?'

Brodie wasn't dumb and resented the question but he had nodded mildly enough. 'Bring back those papers signed by the girl and your bonus'll be a hundred,' the rancher promised.

Brodie had smiled at that. *Yeah, maybe a hundred to start with!* By now, he knew so much about Keefer that he figured it was fast approaching the time when he could demand — and get — a partnership in the Slash K cattle empire. It would be chancy, for Keefer was no man to mess with, but he was also sharp enough to know who was dealing winning cards.

And for a long time, Fergus Keefer hadn't been able to live without the help and co-operation of the man he called his ramrod. *Not for much longer . . .*

Then, as they came out of the cleft between the hills, glad to leave the pulsing heat behind that had been reflecting onto them, Brodie hauled rein.

'The hell's happened there?'

The others followed his pointing finger and saw what he must be indicating: a huge spill of fresh-looking dirt and rocks, spewing from a broken maw in the hillside that looked like a mouth smashed out of shape by some giant fist.

Todd hawked and spat: his comment. Wolf was totally silent but Hazard said,

'Looks like there's been a cave-in.'

'A blind Mexican could see that!' snapped Brodie. He hadn't been expecting anything like this. 'I'm wonderin' how it happened . . . The shaft was loose and dangerous, but it'd need somethin' to make it collapse. It was OK yesterday.'

'Well' — Hazard was puzzled at Brodie's interest — 'it don't matter to us now, does it?'

He fell silent as Brodie's bleak gaze touched him and moved uncomfortably in the saddle. 'It could mean someone's been pokin' around here lookin' for the gal!'

'Oh-oh.' Hazard just had to say *something* but no one paid attention. 'Well, if they was, mebbe they got caught in the rockfall.'

Brodie's turn to grunt as he slid his rifle from his saddle scabbard. Todd and Wolf did the same. Hazard was last, but when they started forward, spreading out at Brodie's signal, he was as ready as the others to shoot first and talk later.

'Ride easy,' Brodie said, in a much quieter voice now. 'Someone — and I mean that son of a bitch Conrad, with help from that goddamn Kidd — just might've figured out I'd stash her in one of these old mine shafts. I want 'em dead! Like the boss said, clean this deal up once and for all. No survivors.'

*   *   *

Ali was badly shaken and couldn't stop rubbing gently at the bite on her left ankle. Conrad had to show her several times before she believed it wasn't a snake bite. A horseshoe of small teeth marks finally convinced her.

'Couldn't see clearly in the tunnel, Ali, but there was a thickish body shape that I took for either a packrat or the front end of a lizard. Lot of 'em head into dark tunnels and caves in the summer, just come out early morning and evening to take the sun and regulate their body temperature.'

She once more examined the small

horseshoe shape of the blood-flecked teeth marks and relaxed some, but her imagination had shaken her up badly.

'I-I thought I was going to die,' she said, her voice still strangely hushed. Her throat was sore from the gag and lack of water and she massaged her neck as she gave Conrad and Kidd a small smile. 'I was so afraid, I-I think I even forgot to pray! I-I've never been so terrified!'

'Don't suppose Brodie said when — or if — he was coming back?'

She shook her head and Conrad stopped pouring canteen water over the bite marks, soaked a strip torn from her petticoat and wrapped the injury firmly.

'We'll have Doc Moreno take a look when we get back to town. Clean it up with antiseptic.'

'Mebbe 'if' we get back?' said Kidd softly. Conrad's head snapped up and he regretted the jerky movement as pain shot through his skull, dimming his vision briefly. Kidd, his rifle in his hand now, nodded to the rise off to the left.

'Somethin' ran across there between the rocks. Was too fast for me to see properly.'

'Big cat?'

'Nope — was a man, I reckon, crouched double, with a rifle. We been found, folks.'

Conrad was already pulling Ali down behind a deadfall where she had sat while he doctored the bite wound. He pushed and thrust her tightly in against the curve of the trunk until she protested.

'Damn you, Russ! I know how to shoot! Give me a gun! I'd just love to get my sights on Brodie!'

He smiled and reached for his six-gun. An instant later a bullet tore bark from the deadfall just beneath his hand as he tossed the revolver over to where Ali lay and dived for cover himself. The whipcrack of the rifle reached him as two more guns opened up and the gulch was filled with echoing gunfire.

Kidd was stretched out amongst

some low rocks, rifle banging, lever working in a blur until he lost the rhythm and a half-ejected shell case jammed the works. He dropped as flat as he could while he worked it free, muttering cusses he hoped Ali wouldn't be able to hear.

'Three of the sonuvers!' he called.

There was a volley of shots from up the slope and, hunched down, Conrad called back, 'Four! The one you thought you saw just bought his two cents' worth!'

Conrad swung up his rifle, winced as a bullet zipped past his face, held his bead and was rewarded with a glimpse — no more than a flash of fabric really — of the killer's shirt. He fired, levered, fired again and a third time. Rock chips spattered, dust spurted and then there was a floundering and an uncoordinated staggering as a man wrenched half upright, blood on his shoulder and neck. Conrad's next bullet exploded the man's head in a pink mist dotted with white pieces of bone. Hazard never knew what hit him.

Ali made a sick sound, but soon after there was the thud of her Colt and a man who had been raising his head up there ducked hurriedly.

'That one you just nailed was Tad Hazard,' Kidd said, loud enough for Conrad to hear above the shooting. The walls threw the gunfire back again and again and it was continuous now. 'Works — *worked* — for Slash K.'

'Then Brodie's up there somewhere!'

As Conrad spoke, crouching as he pushed fresh loads through the spring-backed gate into the under-barrel tubular magazine, he searched, trying to pin down the attackers.

'That looks like Green's old hat!' he said. 'The one with the big dent in it . . .'

'Likely shared his things out amongst the crew at Slash K after they buried him.'

'I saw that hat,' Ali said, unexpectedly, and had to wait for another volley to whine and scream away before she added, 'It's the one described by Cassie Weddemier, worn by the man who killed Calico Bill in the stage hold-up.'

Conrad wasn't really interested, although briefly he wondered why Slash K men would bother holding-up a stage that carried no loot.

'You want to give up, now's the time, Conrad!' Chick Brodie's rough voice suddenly called down the slope. 'We got you pinned. Save yourself some trouble and come out, and grab a handful of sky!'

'Save your breath, Brodie,' Conrad called, squinting as the effort sent fresh pain coursing behind his eyes. 'We both know none of us are going to walk away from this if you have a say in it.'

There was a brief burst of laughter. 'Could be you're right. Only gave you the chance because of the gal. We can use her some before we finish the job.'

Conrad glanced down the length of the deadfall to Ali. He saw her mouth tighten, then she raised up fearlessly and emptied the six-gun in the direction of Brodie's voice. Dirt erupted and lead laid sliver streaks across rocks before ricocheting into the afternoon.

'Whooeeee! Say, she's a hellcat, ain't she? You fellers watch where you're shootin', hear? Don't ruin the merchandise! I got me dibs on that one!'

Conrad fired at Brodie's position, too, knowing the man would be well under cover, but the arrogance and chilling confidence of the man made him mad. Plus his damn headache was worsening with every gunshot. It got much worse, and he'd charge up there like the time with the Texas Brigade at Catskill Bend, risking everything just to end it!

Kidd started shooting, half-lifting when he saw a movement. A man up the slope jerked upright, spinning, and Kidd put one more shot into him as the man fell out of the clump of rocks where he had been hiding, gun flying from his hands. He hit hard, maybe broke his neck, although that wouldn't matter as he was already dead. Then his body slid and rolled and skidded down the slope, stopping only yards above where the trio were dug in. It was Todd.

Then Conrad whipped around to the left as he heard Kidd grunt loudly. The man was hurled back by striking lead and he crashed on to his side on a rock, slid off and jarred heavily to the ground. He had lost his rifle on the far side of the sheltering boulder, out in the open where it could not be retrieved . . . he made no movement. Conrad tightened his lips.

After quickly reloading the Winchster, he took off his gunbelt and tossed it along to the girl.

'Is — is Kidd . . . ?' she asked, tentatively, staring at the unmoving man. Blood showed on his shirt now.

'I dunno,' Conrad snapped, making himself look away and pay attention to the men still above. He swore softly. Damnit to hell! They'd moved and now he didn't know where they were! He'd allowed himself to be distracted.

Crouching close to the deadfall, wishing it was twice as thick, he pushed his hat off and raised his head far enough so his eyes were level with the top of the log. Then raised it another inch. Instantly a bullet thudded into the wood and he dropped, half-blinded by bits of flying bark. *The white patch of lint made too good a target!*

Clawing at his face, he asked the girl in a harsh whisper, 'You see where that came from?'

She hesitated. 'My God! That was a dangerous thing to do, drawing their fire that way!'

'*Did you see where it came from?*' he repeated, hard voiced now.

'I — think — there! By the yucca! I can see a piece of shirt caught on the pointed leaves . . .'

'Stay down!' Conrad yelled as, in her excitement, she started to rise, bringing the Colt up.

A gun slammed and Ali gave a cry, her slim body twisted, rolling in a cascade of skirts and colour as she landed face down one arm outstretched — the six-gun lying on its side in the dust.

Without conscious thought, Conrad was on his feet in an instant, a rebel yell bursting from his lungs as he leapt over the deadfall and ran forward, zig-zagging, crouching, rifle butt against his hip, lever and trigger working.

His bullets raked the yucca plant, soggy leaves and sap spraying. There was a floundering and thrashing and a hard-faced man he'd never seen before, reared up, trying to bring his own rifle around. Conrad triggered again and the bullet took Wolf through the middle of the face, knocking him flat.

Panting, Conrad slowed, realizing the foolishness of his move now, leaving himself exposed in the open like this —

A rifle whiplashed and his right leg kicked out from under him and he went down on one knee. He brought his own rifle up, triggering one-handed, but the hammer fell on an empty breech and he let the smoking weapon sag slowly as he watched a grinning Chick Brodie stand up slowly, covering him.

'Got you just where I want you at last, drifter! Dead where you stand, right? Damn Wolf shootin' the gal, though! But mebbe she's got some life left in her yet . . . ' His smile took on a mean, crooked look. 'Might just leave you alive for a spell so's you can watch — you like that, Conrad?'

'What I'd like — is — to see you knocked flat with the life draining out of you,' Conrad gritted.

'Never happen! Second thoughts, I don't think I'll let you live another ten seconds. *Adios*, you son of a bitch! The trouble you've caused me!'

He lifted his rifle to his shoulder and Conrad tensed, ready to throw himself sideways and down-slope. With any luck he would skid close enough to pick up his Colt dropped by Ali and . . .

The shot slapped at his ears in mid-thought and for a second he wondered why he hadn't felt the impact of the bullet.

Then he saw Chick Brodie was down, slumping body spilling over the low rocks to sprawl on his back. Blood was running from a wound above his right eye and Conrad knew there would be no recovery from *that*.

He lifted his gaze, surprised to see Brad Tyrell standing on top of the ridge, looking down, smoking rifle held across his chest. He gestured to Brodie's body.

'You got your wish, Conrad.'

Conrad lifted a hand in acknowledgement and then a wave of dizziness swept over him and he felt himself tumbling into darkness . . .

* * *

Ali was all right. The bullet had struck the rock beside her and a piece had smacked her lower leg, penetrating Conrad's crude bandage, kicking her leg from under her. When she'd fallen, she had hit her head hard knocking herself cold instantly.

She was still groggy, but bound up the wound in Conrad's leg which, luckily, did not involve any broken bones.

Brad Tyrell came back from examining Kidd. He shook his head at Conrad's enquiring look. Conrad remained deadpan.

'I should've been here earlier, but I lost their tracks.' Both Conrad and the girl gave him puzzled looks. 'I went to see Keefer. They gave me a lot of malarkey about what had happened and I knew I wasn't going to get any good sense out of them. So I made out I was satisfied with their story and left. Only I waited and sure enough Brodie came riding out with three of his hardcases. I followed but lost their trail. Then I heard the shooting and came as fast as I could.'

'We're very glad to see you, Brad,' Ali told him, smiling. 'I think you'll find Keefer ordered the stage hold-up. I'd mentioned the copy of the records of Russ filing on Two-way Creek was being despatched to the Land Agency in Austin — that's what he was after, to destroy all evidence of the land ever having been filed-on officially.'

Brad nodded. 'Yes. On Brodie's body I found some land claim forms filled out in Keefer's name. Just needed your signature as 'witness' to make them legal, Ali.'

'So that's why they came back for me! Well, that should be enough, Brad, enough to involve Keefer so you can arrest him. Because those forms had to have come from my office; that's the only place you can get them. And that means Keefer sent someone to break in and steal the forms. His name and signature already on them is a dead giveaway.'

The sheriff smiled widely. 'Sis, you're right! Keefer's finished! The only land he's going to be interested in for the next twenty years is the rockpile in Fort Worth's Penitentiary.'

Ali turned her grimy face towards Conrad who thought she looked fine, dirt and all. 'How about you, Russ?'

'Well, if that land at Two-way Creek is still available for prove-up — '

'It is! I can guarantee it!' she told him quickly.

He shrugged. 'Gimme a coupla weeks to get back on my feet — literally! — and I'm your man.'

She sobered, and then there was a twinkle in her eyes as she said, smiling once more, 'Yes, I'd like that, Russ Conrad — you being my man.'

That wasn't quite what he meant! But she had given him a clear-enough message.

He gave it a moment's thought: that's all it took.

He wasn't sure how Brad felt about that, but Conrad himself didn't mind.

Not one bit.

Other titles in the
Linford Western Library:

ESCAPE FROM FORT BENTON

Scott Connor

Nathan Palmer and Jeff Morgan happen across the victim of an ambush. The dying man gives them a cryptic message about ten thousand dollars being available in Fort Benton in five days' time. However, arriving at Fort Benton to get the money, they come up against Mayor Decker and his ruthless form of justice. Soon the pair are beaten up and thrown in jail. In Decker's clutches, they're going to need all their courage if they are ever to escape.

TRAITOR'S GOLD

Wade Dellman

Marshal Dave Stevens' mission was to capture the outlaw Ned Bartell, a traitor who had caused the deaths of two thousand of his fellow Confederate soldiers during the Civil War. Pinkerton operative Marie Devlin, whose dead brother Bartell had betrayed, and ex-army veteran Thorpe also wanted Bartell brought to justice. Bartell's greed for gold brought Stevens, Thorpe and the girl together — but would their combined resolve still be enough to ensure their survival against the vicious outlaws?